Containers For Death

CONTAINERS FOR DEATH

Gregory C. Randall

Amazon Version

Printed in the United States of America

Windsor Hill Publishing, Inc.
Walnut Creek, California 94596

ISBN: 978-0-9828376-3-4

This book is dedicated to my father, John C. Randall, who taught me all things are possible.

Chapter 1

The line cut through the following sea like a strand of silk through Listerine-colored water. High behind the stern of the forty-year-old slug of fiberglass, the desert wind blew the foam off the wave's crest in ragged strips, where, inside the wall of gargling water, dark shapes danced, backlit by the sun. The doorknob exploded from the face of the blue cliff, throwing slack into the line, quickly made taut by the charging boat. The knob bounced twice off the tepid sea, throwing spray in all directions, before it dug itself back into the ocean. A split second passed, then two dark shapes turned and exploded out of the blue wall and surfed down the face of the wave, their swords slashing left and right, trying to murder the orange doorknob. A rooster tail of seawater sprayed from the line as it again came taut; the marlin—their dorsal fins erect—charged the lure.

"Señorita, ally. There, there. Hold the tip up, drag—watch the drag."

"Not my first rodeo, Gregorio. I see them."

Sharon O'Mara jumped from the fighting chair, slammed the butt of the rod into the gimbal on the leather belt strapped to her full hips, gulped hot air, and braced herself. Jesus, the deck hand, cinched up the buckles.

"Gracias, Jesus. Gracias."

"She is coming, Señorita, there, there. Be ready!" Gregorio yelled from the makeshift deck and tower attached to the top of the old cabin, like a stainless-steel Mexican tree house. "She is rising."

Sharon held the rod loose and studied the wake in the following sea as it rose full high on the next wave. Jesus yelled something to the captain and pointed at the wave; Gregorio grimaced and nudged the throttle a bit. The boat climbed the next wave and, at its peak, she could see two, then three, torpedo shapes attack the lure; their swords slashed at the knob, each trying to beat the other to the orange chunk of plastic. They pushed each other aside and charged; their heads thrashed the ocean, spray exploded. The largest crashed through the chaos, knocked away the contenders, and ripped through the cobalt water straight into the lure's path and snagged it. Sharon's reel began to sing the song of a thousand nails being dragged across a thousand blackboards. She turned to Gregorio, backlit by the sun, she—blinded by the glare.

"Now, now, now, rapido, rapido, go!" she screamed.

The Cummins diesel roared and the boat charged forward down the face of the wave; Sharon locked the reel and struck the fish. Again the line cut through the wall of ocean rising up behind the boat, but now it carved a slash across the sea to the right. The black marlin's shape held in the clearness of the wave like it had been caught in one of those cheap Lucite blocks holding spiders and scorpions and other stuff, but this was not Lucite and this was not dead; this was 525 pounds of very pissed-off fish. Sharon braced her hips against the rail and heard the line scream out as it chased the fish, hoping the 850 yards of monofilament line would be enough. Gregorio, sensing her thoughts, turned the boat to parallel the flight path of the fish as it jumped once, then twice, and then, on the third leap, appeared to hold itself in the air for so long that Michael Jordan would want to trade in his face on a Wheaties box for the chance to float that high for that long and that wonderfully. When the marlin stopped being an eagle, to again become a fish, a hole opened in the Sea of Cortez and she sounded.

1b

Sharon slept for two days straight with only brief stints at the breakfast table, dinner table, and the bar. The bullet holes were pink scars now, but only scabs a week before; the mental scars were being slowly washed away by piña coladas and Black

Label, not together, but separately and with ample amounts of Bohemia to ensure a modicum of space between the two. There were no nightmares, no cold sweats, and no regrets, other than having to leave her live-in boyfriend at the kennel. Kevin Bryan was staying with his mother in San Francisco for the past week, so Basil lost his usual second home for the few weeks that she was on the East Cape in Baja.

"R and R—just like in Iraq," she told herself. "Fight like hell for three weeks, get two days off, and then back into the furnace. Maybe that's why I like this part of Mexico, hot and dry and clean. Compared to Iraq, two out of three ain't bad, and the food and the fishing is fantastic. Iraqi goat was never my favorite, no matter how it was cooked. A carnitas enchilada, covered in guacamole, cheese, and sour cream is all I need to get by, that and a tequila shooter or two."

After the thing in Lafayette with the Clayburn Company and the serious fuckup that resulted in her being fired and the three weeks in the hospital with the hole in her leg that was trying to close up, she regained enough sanity to realize that she needed to get away. She wanted to get far enough away where cell phones didn't work and there was nothing on TV in the room because there was no TV in the room. She needed warm water, dry nights, a handy bar, a trashy book, and fish, big fish, fish that would eat you for lunch or, at the very least, try to kill you for disturbing their peaceful life of terrorizing sardines and mackerel.

Sharon remembered the first few times she came to this side of Baja and the East Cape, dirt roads, no air-conditioning, great food, clean water, cold beer, and no tourists. The ocean, hers and the boat's for days at a time, no others, and about a quarter of what charters cost in Hawaii and without the big seas. Baja offered a horizon uninterrupted by the spikes of outriggers and towers, where, when you had a fish on, no one would pull up to watch, or try to parallel the run to snag one of the others in the school. Those days were gone now. Now there were huge PG&E-like towers on the boats, air-conditioned rooms, fancy onyx-tiled washrooms on the golf courses, and goddamned well-oiled and sun-burned tourists in tony gear, silly hats, 36 handicaps, fat wives, fat boyfriends, too much tequila, flabby cruising day-trippers, and all (soon to have Montezuma's revenge churning their stomachs) turistas.

She needed a new business plan, and only in Cabo, she assured herself, could she find it. She needed a clear head, sometimes, a clean room, maybe, and mostly only herself for as long as it took. She established a daily program for herself, consisting of getting up early, having a shot of juice, taking a run down the beach (that used to be a runway where Crosby and his cronies would fly into to dry out), going fishing, eating dinner, and the next day—doing it again.

And it's working, she thought. The stiffness in the leg was loosening up and she felt a lot healthier than the days she had spent with a bitchy physical therapist, and besides, the view was ten times better. A week of her personal therapy had bronzed her Irish hide, pushed up the graying roots of her red hair, and had put two yellowfin tuna, one sailfish, and a thirty-pound roosterfish on her caught-and-released list, or at least the sailfish and the roosterfish made the list; the tuna were the proud dinner guests that night, along with their dates of butter and cilantro.

She leaned toward freelancing, a helper of those needing help. Kevin already suggested a few things with some kids with family problems.

"Just what I need, more family problems, me, an orphan who has lived a hundred miles from any kind of family structure," she said to Kevin. "The only nuclear family I know is what I see on TV—I don't think so. I need to make a living, not just scratch by, real dinero, real dollars. I have special talents and, with some of the connections I have, maybe I can get a gig or two. I might go into salvage, find lost stuff, and maybe even become a Travis McGee with tits."

"And a nice ass, but that will only get you the kind of work that requires nights, not days, and, if I remember correctly, you're an early morning gal," Kevin added, with a leer.

"I'll slap that grin off your face," Sharon said, with a matching smirk. "No, I'm serious; people lose things all the time, sometimes stolen things, sometimes lost things, and even sometimes illegal things. There may be a few who would pay well to get them back."

"Kind of close to the edge," Kevin added. "Wrong guess and you're on the opposite side of me. That's someplace I don't want you to be."

"Vetting, it's all about vetting and investigation. No handshakes, no verbal promises, all contractual with signatures and retainers. McGee got deals where he kept half of the recovery—most of the time it was half of nothing and that's nothing in my book. I want an hourly plus expenses; so if the check bounces, I leave. I'm paid weekly or it's adios Sharon. Besides, I will run, breathless, to you to vet anything that smells and then only if the money makes it worth the risk. And the client will know it."

Kevin Bryan only shook his head and muttered something about settling down or some other inanity. Sharon crooked her head and laughed.

1c

The rod tip pointed almost straight down and line kept running into the deep canyon, a thousand feet under the keel. She slowly turned the drag, putting more and more pressure on the rod, the line, and the hook.

"Señorita, please be careful, don't want to lose her," Jesus said, softly.

"I won't; just a bit to slow her down, just a half turn."

It began to work; the fish slowed his decent, then held—like a tuna. Sharon slowly raised the rod, nothing. Again she pulled, and again nothing. Then the tip went stiff, like it had just sat down at a strip club; the limp line started to pool on the ocean's surface.

"Gregorio, now, now, now!" Sharon reeled in as fast she could, knuckles just missing the rail. Gregorio gunned the boat to pick up the line's slack. The bend returned to the rod and she continued to gain line, maybe a hundred yards still spooled out. A seagull, seeing something, dipped and carved a sharp curve over the water; a spray of sardines exploded from the trough between the waves, followed by the biggest goddamn fish Sharon O'Mara had ever seen.

"Madre Dios," muttered Jesus. "She is one big feesh."

Sharon pulled hard and the black head thrashed and frothed the water with its sword. Sardines flew in great handfuls from the surface; more birds appeared from out of nowhere and dived on the bait. The ocean churned with small fish, predators, and seabirds.

"Frenzy in the middle of all this, what a fantastic sight," she said, scanning the roiling surface, the rod still taut to the fish.

Every once in a while, if enough time is spent on the fertile areas of the seas, the lucky mariner may happen on one of nature's most spectacular and chaotic mass murders. When bait fish are pushed to the surface by predators, such as tuna and maybe dolphin (the mammal, not the fish), and are set upon by seagulls, pelicans, and terns that gorge themselves until the bait runs out or escapes, there may not be one single bait fish alive in that frothy melee. Her marlin charged up from the deep ocean into the middle of this feeding frenzy and added to the anarchy and it was every fish for himself, total madness.

She slowly worked her fish to the boat, and then it would run again, and then get reeled back in. Seagulls still screamed across the sky, but the frenzy had moved away. She glanced at her watch. An hour had gone by, the longest she ever fought a fish. Jesus handed her a beer; it disappeared as fast as she could breathe it in. It felt wonderful, even though the sinews in her arms were shrieking. The reel was now held close to her hips with a back brace and harness as she took a second to shake out her arms. She would have one hellava bruise tomorrow circling her waist; the rod dipped, and the line screamed again.

"Shit."

"She dives again, Señorita, maybe not so deep this time," Jesus hoped.

Again the play began, third act, usually the last, but sometimes playwrights can be tricky and will fool with you. Again the pull, then reel, pull then reel in, crank the son of a bitch until either your arm or the leader breaks the surface, pull the rod, and then reel. Jesus laid a wet towel over her head.

"Gracias."

Swivel, leader, and wire broke the surface. Sharon looked back up to the bridge.

"Gregorio, let's get her in now and tag her. She deserves to live."

"Si, Señorita, that she does," he answered from overhead.

He slammed the boat into reverse and backed down on the fish; she held the black marlin in place and reeled to take up the slack, as the boat pushed backwards. A wave churned over the transom, drenching Jesus and Sharon with refreshing seawater.

Jesus grabbed the tagging stick with the release tag locked to its tip. The fish slowly carved its way to the side of the boat; exhaustion held tightly at both ends of the line. The black-on-black flanks rippled electrically along the side of the fish, flashing its excitement and anger. The billfish rolled an eye up toward its tormentor; Sharon stared back at the giant.

"How long?" she yelled to Gregorio, now standing next to her, the wire leader wrapped around a heavy leather glove.

"Eight feet, with bill, eleven," he answered. "Maybe five hundred pounds, maybe more."

"Tag her."

"You sure? She's a good fish. Mucho dollars."

"No, tag her. Her children will give you work for years, *comprendes*?"

"Si, but she would be the biggest of the year," the captain said with a smile.

"Yes, and you are the big cock at the dock. No, tag her, let her go."

Gregorio yelled toward Jesus, who leaned over the transom and stuck the tag below the dorsal fin, then grabbed the bill of the fish while Gregorio pulled the hook from the jaw, and, as he held onto the sword, he could feel the fish strengthen, its power returning. He released the bill just as Sharon clicked pictures with her camera. The giant hovered, then slowly sank and disappeared into the blue black of the ocean.

The captain turned to Sharon with a huge smile. She returned the grin and yelled "Bueno, bueno," and stuck out her tired hand to get a handshake.

Sharon watched as the captain's face turned white, the grin gone, only panic staring back at her. He leaped to the ladder and up to the bridge, gunned the throttle, and spun the wheel to the right. The hard turn knocked Jesus to the deck. Sharon held on to the rail, the only thing keeping her from joining the marlin, and watched the massive red box skim by the rail of the boat with letters three feet high announcing its name to all: PCL.

Chapter 2

Gregorio eased the boat in a large arc and approached the shipping container from the port side, put the boat in idle, and jumped to the deck.

"You okay, Señorita O'Mara?" he asked.

Sharon sat down into the fighting chair, felt her arms, and ran her fingers through her sweaty hair.

"Yes, Gregorio, I'm okay, nothing broken. Check Jesus."

The deckhand lay facedown, blood from the gash on his forehead mixed with the seawater sloshing about the deck. Sharon slowly rolled the boy over and held a towel to his head. Jesus opened his eyes.

"Just a small cut, must have caught a bit of the rail when he went down. You okay?"

Jesus blinked and a big smiled opened up his face. "Si. Okay, okay. I'm *muy fuerte.*"

"Yes, Jesus, you're strong, but let's see that cut," Sharon said.

She took a good look, not deep, just messy, maybe a stitch or two when they got in. She ripped open a gauze pad from the first-aid box and then wrapped a strip of bandage around his head to hold it in place.

"Too sweaty to hold a Band-Aid; now you look like a revolucionario."

Jesus grinned, then looked at the red box bobbing in the ocean. He turned to Gregorio.

"What do you think, Captain? She maybe ours? Maybe our turn for Christmas in *Junio,* maybe?"

Gregorio smiled and thought for a moment. "What do you think, Señorita? Maybe we put a rope on that thing, maybe we call another boat over, maybe we tow it to the beach, and maybe we look and see what she has inside? Maybe nothing. See, she rides real high; maybe, then again, it may be Christmas."

Sharon O'Mara looked at the nine-foot-high shipping container and wondered. It was riding high, which meant it had a good seal, and no water inside. Whatever was in there was light and not pushing the box deeper into the sea. She had heard about boxes being lost or falling overboard; she never believed it, though. Hell, they weighed a couple of tons, so they had to sink. But here it was, floating around like the biggest bobber a fisherman could ever use and it certainly was not her place to tell these two what was right or wrong; life was a bitch for them and their families. Besides, there might be something in there that they could turn a profit from; a few pesos for the niños would not hurt.

"Si, let's tow it in, but the clock is stopped, okay?"

Gregorio smiled. "Si, the clock, she is stopped. Let's see what we can find."

The captain climbed up the ladder and pulled the radio mike off the wall, and, with the gusto only an excited Mexican fisherman can show, spoke briefly. He put the boat in gear and slowly moved to intersect the container. Jesus, anticipating the move, climbed up from the cramped and squalid lower cabin dragging a hemp hawser line at least an inch thick. Sharon looked at the line and smiled — always be prepared was her motto.

Gregorio maneuvered the boat alongside and slowly inched the craft to the double door end of the box; a large padlock under the cover plate secured the door, and what looked like a custom's seal and wire hung across the opening. Jesus played out twenty feet of the hawser, dove in, and secured the line to the box at each corner.

"Good job, Jesus. *Muy bien, bravo*," Gregorio said as Jesus climbed back onboard. "Now we wait for Esteban and the *Flying Fish*; he said he would be here in about thirty minutes. He is alone with Roberto, no fishing today, testing out the refit on the boat. He is a good man."

"Si, he is your brother," Jesus said with a big grin.

Sharon wrapped a new bandage around Jesus's head. Gregorio went below for a minute and returned with a short-handled axe.

"Señorita, if that box starts to sink, you cut that line pronto. I don't want her pulling us to the bottom of the sea where the fish can get even for all the evil things I have done to them over the years, si?"

Sharon smiled. "Si, my name is also on that list, Gregorio."

Gregorio climbed up to the cabin, maneuvered the boat in front of the box, and slowly accelerated. The line, secured to the large transom cleats, became taught, almost to the breaking point, and then, as they defeated inertia, the box began to move in their direction. The seas had flattened considerably since the fight with the marlin—they were in the lee of the mountains now and, at about two knots an hour, headed toward shore.

At about the thirty-minute mark, Esteban and the *Flying Fish* pulled alongside and they conducted the same ballet. Gregorio took the lead position and his brother, immediately and to one side, followed in his wake. The speed ramped to about four knots.

"*Quanto tiempo,*" Sharon yelled up to Gregorio.

"Maybe two hours, if we are lucky," he answered. "Señorita, why not fish? We are not going fast and there may be a dorado or two under that thing."

If anything floats in the warm waters of the ocean—a lost icebox, a raft of debris, a lost shipping container—it's almost guaranteed to attract small baitfish seeking the shade. This also attracts predators as well, especially the spectacular dorado or mahi-mahi, as it's called in the Sandwich Islands. Jesus rigged Sharon's saltwater fly rod with one of the gaudiest lures in her tackle box, smiled, and handed the long stick to her. Taking a position on the side away from the *Flying Fish*, she slowly pumped the line out to almost seventy-five feet before she let it hit the surface with a delicate splash. She let it sit two heartbeats and began to quickly strip the line in with three-foot pulls, while the feathers danced and jerked in the clear water. Her eye caught a flash to her right and a golden-green mirror slashed through the water, launched itself into the air, and caught the fly in mid-pull. The line ripped from Sharon's fingers. In a second, she stood fast into a high-speed freight train headed for Mazatlan. Her hand acted like a break on the reel's rim. The fish, easily twenty pounds, immediately somersaulted ten times as it jive-danced across the Sea of Cortez, like it was trying out for *Dancing with the Stars*, doing everything to throw the yellow-orange lure back in Sharon's eye.

Sharon lifted the rod's tip and pointed it toward the fish as it started another run, this time toward the container and the tow lines. She turned the head of the dorado and worked it forward and away from the box. Standing on the bow, she had more room to maneuver and control the jumping, flying, tail-walking, and just plain overly pissed-off game fish. Three more runs and it was done. Sharon walked the dorado to the stern where Jesus remained with the axe. She looked over the side and saw at least six more rockets zipping back and forth under the boat, all trying to give aid and comfort to their soon-to-be-lost associate. A swift jerk of the gaff brought the fish to the deck; the camp followers disappeared into the dark blue. A sharp whack from the bat, an old Louisville slugger, quickly quieted the fish.

"Gracias, Jesus, bueno, a good fish and a good dinner. Put him on ice, okay."

"Si, Señorita O'Mara. You use that silly long stick pretty good. Si, very good."

For the next two hours they worked their way toward the beach, and the wind died to nothing. Fighting waves and a high wind would have made the haul almost impossible. Two more boats came alongside but no more lines were added; Gregorio didn't want to stop until they reached the shore.

Along the East Cape, known for its rugged mountains and quiet beaches, there are no harbors like those found at San Jose and Cabo San Lucas. Here the boats are tied to floats secured to old car engines idling on the sandy bottom. When a boat needs refitting, or more substantial work, it's floated onto a cradle then hauled up a railroad-like ramp on the beach. An old truck engine runs a winch with a steel cable. This is what Gregorio had in mind for the box; it would be floated over the cradle and slowly dragged up the rails onto the beach.

Two more boats put stabilizing lines on the box to counter the freshening afternoon breeze as they positioned the container over the rails. Jesus swam to the double-door end, untied the towlines, and attached the winch cable. A wave of his arm signaled "start the engine," and noisily the winch began its work. The box grounded on the cradle after five feet and slowly the container rose out of the ocean, and after riding fifteen feet, it sat dry, dripping saltwater. Jesus signaled to stop and removed the lines. Gregorio moved his boat to its mooring and transferred O'Mara's gear to the waiting rowboat. Ten minutes later, everything sat on the beach; the fish was on its way to the kitchen, the tackle was being washed by the pool, and there were thirty expectant people standing along the ramp edge.

Tools appeared: a small sledgehammer, a large pair of bolt cutters, and a cutting torch. Gregorio snipped off the heavy wire of the customs tag and then took the torch and made short work of the protective bracket covering the lock. A short whack of the sledge broke away the cover, and, with one motion, the bolt cutter clipped through the large padlock securing the doors.

"Señorita, it's maybe Christmas now," Jesus said to Sharon, with the biggest grin she had seen all day.

Gregorio released the four latches and began to slowly open the right side door. It stuck. He banged on the door with the sledge, pulled hard, and the doors exploded outward, throwing him to the sand onto his back; a nasty cut bled above his left eye. The closest men doubled over and retched, a young woman quickly gathered her children and ran up the beach, another crossed herself and fell to her knees. Jesus, engulfed in the stench, threw up; a woman quickly ran to Gregorio's side and used her full skirt to staunch the blood trickling down his face.

Sharon's nose told her exactly what was in the box as years in Iraq ingrained the senses with things beyond what you want to remember from day to day. You never forget the stench of rotting human flesh. She looked inside and the dark interior gave a backdrop to the bright sunshine falling on the four male corpses hanging from a makeshift horizontal bar welded to the box.

As much as she didn't want them to, Sharon's police skills kicked in. She placed a towel over her mouth and immediately began to assess what she saw inside: the box's interior, the cardboard boxes behind the corpses, the ropes, the clothes, everything. Then, to only make matters worse, one body broke away from its head and crashed to the floor. The head sat for a long second entangled in the noose, then fell to the deck with a thud, bounced once, and fell to the sand between the rails, its vacant eye sockets staring up for one last look at the sun.

2b

Sharon quickly closed the door, secured the latches, placed a towel over the sand-covered head, and backed away. A well-dressed man ran up to her from the general direction of the hotel.

"Señorita O'Mara, what has happened? I have told these people not to drag these things here. Take them somewhere else I tell them, I don't care. But not here, not on the hacienda's beach, too much trouble, too much police," the manager said, in a panic.

"Well, Señor Valdez, we are well beyond that now. It's here, it's going nowhere, and the police, I'm sure, will be here like the flies that are already buzzing about. Nothing brings out the police like dead bodies."

"Madre Dios. Si, they have been called. Will be here in an hour; they have to come up from San Jose." Valdez looked at the red box. "Anything we can do?" He was clearly hoping there was nothing needed from him.

"No, Señor Valdez, those men are going nowhere. Just keep the dogs away from that towel."

"Towel?"

"Yes, that towel, we don't want them taking away the head that sits under it for a snack."

Valdez's tanned brown skin visibly whitened and he started to get very, very sick.

"Turn away from the box, take a deep breath, and go back to your office; there will be more calls. Put that one lazy security guard you have out here to keep away the gawkers."

"Ga-awkers?"

"*Turistas. Comprendes?*"

'Si, yes, to keep away the ga-awkers."

The crowd quickly dispersed once they saw Señor Valdez; most of them wanted to be somewhere else. The police would ask questions and that would take time from their jobs and, for that, Valdez would dock their pay. Sharon scanned the beach and saw Gregorio and Jesus talking with Ernesto and wondered what was going on. Spotting a lone beach chair under an umbrella, she pulled a beer from the boat's cooler, sat down in the shade, lit a Marlboro, and inhaled.

"Well, this has been a fun day," she said out loud to no one. "We caught a blue marlin, a dorado, and four dead hombres. We released one, kept one, and put the rest back in the box. Just great!"

She blew smoke toward the red container with the large PCL letters painted on its side; the three white letters sat within a double-lined box obviously representing a container enclosing the letters. She also noticed the box's other lettering and numbers on its side and on the doors: tariff info, maximum weight, capacity, and, obviously, the shipping line. Smaller letters spelled out "Pacific Container Line" on the lower panel of the door. Up the beach from where she sat, three other rusty boxes, embedded in the sand, and used for storage by the hotel for the boats and beach gear, were secured to large chains running up the hill to hooks set deep into the rock. Smiling, she remembered that even ten-ton boxes would float away when the surge from a hurricane runs up the beach.

"Señorita, can I get you something to drink? "

"*Buenos tardes, Jose. Si, uno margarita,*" she answered. The beer was warm—a frozen tequila seemed mucho better.

"Si, Señorita O'Mara, one margarita." Jose stood looking at the box.

"You okay?" Sharon asked.

"Si, but this reminds me of my home up north in Tijuana, death and dead lying in alleys and along the roads, all due to drugs. That's why I came here, to get away from all that and to raise my son where such things don't happen. But they follow, even here, to this place that's away from everywhere. They say they were hanging from ropes?"

"Yes, Jose, they were and still are. Obviously they were sent as a message from wherever they were to wherever it was going, a scary and brutally blunt message. I have no idea what happened or where it was going, maybe the police can figure it out."

"Maybe. But soon you will meet Captain Lopez and you will not be that confident. He isn't the same kind of policeman you have up north; he is, as you say, very independent and procedures are things to avoid, like paperwork. So, be aware, and besides, Señorita, if I may, he also fancies himself to be a Mexican Casanova," Jose said with a wink.

"Jose, that'll be easier to deal with than his incompetence. My guess is the crime scene is obviously somewhere else, but the box's insides will probably be trashed before this is all over. The hotel will want the bodies away from here as soon as possible and the box put on a truck so that by tomorrow the beach will be clear. Señor Valdez wants that more than anything."

"Si, I will be right back with your margarita."

Sharon watched Jose climb the stairs to the hotel bar extending out on a large stone terrace toward the Sea of Cortez. Palms hid the lower stone rip-rap stacked to fend off the high surf pushed in by storms. Peeking out between the fronds, the gawkers stood with their fruit drinks, mini-umbrellas, Tommy shirts, shorts, and sunburned legs. Instinctively, they all knew to stay away, but felt safe enough to watch from on high, like they were at a sporting event or at the theater.

The margarita arrived. Jose said that he needed to get back to the bar. Señor Valdez noticed that he had done more than just take her drink order and cautioned against further conversations. She told Jose that she understood, and maybe they would talk later. She lit another cigarette.

"Señorita, I'm very sorry this has happened," Gregorio offered, as he walked up to her. "We thought maybe the box would have things we could use or maybe sell; no one cares down here when someone finds these things. Last year, my cousin towed one in and there were enough clothes for everyone in the village and some to sell in town. I heard that one dragged in up near La Paz had TVs in it. The captain made a lot of money with that one, so I think, maybe it's Christmas for me and my family. She now has only brought trouble." He hooked his fist and thumb toward the container. "She is now a gigante pain in the ass." He turned and headed toward Jesus and his brother.

Sharon was into her second margarita when she heard the distant intermittent scream of a police siren, echoing off the hot stone cliffs standing above the hotel. Only the ledge, cut for the road, separated the complex from the hundred feet of vertical rock and the hundred miles of desert that ran west until it plunged into the Pacific Ocean. Sharon watched the two squad cars slide down the gravel road to the hotel, followed by a large step-van with "GUARDIA" written in bold white letters on the dark green paint, a dust cloud following in their wake.

2c

Inspector Detective Xavier Immanuel Lopez paraded down the stone stairs from the hotel parking lot, looking like a refugee from the movie *Evita*. His entourage followed. His military-cut uniform was obviously not standard police issue and the high-billed cap looked like it had been stolen from Juan Peron. The braiding on the shoulders only added to the comic look and required Sharon to restrain every facial muscle, trying not to break out in a huge grin. She crushed her cigarette just as Inspector Lopez stopped, looked over the scene, pulled a silver case from his coat pocket, and lit a small cigar. Not missing the fact that the only woman on the beach was Sharon, he marched directly to her, tried to click his heels in the sand, and bowed sharply.

"*Buenos tardes, Señorita*. I'm Inspector Detective Lopez with the Baja Sur Guardia. May I offer you my card, please? And you are?"

Sharon continued, with difficulty, to restrain herself. She took his card, glanced at it, noting that it was in both Spanish and English. "I'm Sharon O'Mara, from California, here on vacation to do some fishing. That's the biggest thing we caught today." She pointed toward the box.

"Four very dead men inside, one head between the rails, there," she continued. "It fell out after the door was opened. That's all anyone here knows for sure. The box was found floating about ten miles off the coast; a couple of the boys thought there would be some treasure inside so they hauled it in. Probably won't be doing that for a while. As far as I can see, the crime scene, as it is, is all inside that box. Not much else on the outside, other than the writing."

"Señorita O'Mara, I will determine what's important."

"Inspector, certainly, it's all yours."

"Señorita O'Mara," Lopez said, as his eyes undressed her up and down with the look of someone at a market. "Excellent. Shall we take a look?"

"Be my guest, there isn't much to add to what I just told you. There might be something in the boxes stashed in with the bodies, but for now I'm staying right here." She smiled.

During their conversation, four policemen joined them after dropping bags of gear. One bag held a camera. Lopez pointed to the box, and told him to shoot the exterior and the doors. He made his way to the rails, the cameraman took pictures of the towel, and, after it had been removed, the head. They slowly opened the doors, and, after five seconds, two of the officers went quickly around behind the box and threw up. Lopez pulled a handkerchief from his back pocket and put it over his nose and mouth. The camera flashed as more photos were taken. The beach had darkened considerably after the sun went behind the mountain. Curiosity got the better of Sharon; she lit another

Marlboro and walked over to the police.

The three bodies still hung on thick white cords, not heavy ropes, secured to the bar; the toes of their bare feet just touched the floor, and the headless fourth lay like a bundle of rags. She looked closely at the bar, the cords, and the men. Strange, she thought, that since the box was maybe eight feet high inside, and the bar was about a foot from the top, and, with the cord lengths, these men could not have been hanged in the usual way by breaking their necks with a drop. They had to have been strangled. All wore jeans and tee shirts, no watches or other jewelry, except one had an earring, a gold loop on his right ear. All were tattooed on their arms, gang style, and had no shoes on. They all had thick heads of stringy black hair; two had beards. From their look and the probable conditions in the box, they had been dead at least a week or more. The cord had sawn through the neck of the one fellow, breaking away his head, and the noose still hung from the bar. Sharon looked at the head on the sand; the cameraman was still taking pictures, and she noticed a small hole just above the right eye. He had been shot, small caliber, maybe a .22 or something else, too small for a 9 mm.

"Inspector Lopez, can you see if the others had been shot in the forehead?"

"Que?" Lopez looked down at her. "What? Foreheads?"

"Yes, this fellow here." She pointed at the head. "Was shot. If the others were also shot, then it looks like they were strung up after they were dead."

Lopez climbed up to the box and, steadying his hand on the side, lifted the hair from the face of the closest body. "Si, this hombre has a very neat hole just above his right eye. Makes some sense. Hard to hang someone like this without a serious fight, especially four of them. They all have their hands tied with the same cord as the nooses. "

The cameraman continued taking photos of the bodies, this time focusing on the hands and faces. Sharon easily saw the boxes stacked immediately behind the bodies; orange plastic netting secured to the walls kept them in place, no labels were visible.

Two more men joined the group, one in an official-looking uniform, but not a policeman's uniform.

"Inspector Lopez?" the man asked. Sharon pointed at Lopez, who continued to look inside the container beyond the bodies.

"Si," Lopez answered. "Coroner?"

"Si, Ernesto Rivera, his assistant."

"Magnifico, the real coroner isn't here and he sends this boy. Great. Where the hell is he?"

"In San Lucas with the body of a dead tourist from a cruise ship, needs to process the body and have it flown back to Los Angeles so the boat can leave. He said, 'Muy importante . . . we need to make sure the cruise ships still come here, even if they drop off dead bodies.'"

"Estupendo, just great. We are almost through here. One of my men will help with the bodies, and then we can haul this thing out of here. Pablo, did you call for a truck to move this box."

"Si, will be here tomorrow."

"Tomorrow. Madre Dios, see what I have to deal with, Miss O'Mara? Incompetence everywhere I turn. Why tomorrow?"

"He is hauling containers for the fish company, and they need to get them to the processor or they will spoil. He will be here tomorrow by nine. He is the only one with a cable and tow winch strong enough to pull the box onto the flatbed. Tomorrow."

"You will stay here until then, and I don't want to hear that you have been up to the bar, si?"

"Si." Pablo looked up at the bar with its fifty heads looking through the palm trees, and sighed.

Sharon shook her head over the messy police work and ongoing contamination and watched Lopez put his ungloved hands against the interior walls of the box and walk through the litter and debris on the floor. Then, to make it worse, the young coroner climbed in, adding his fingerprints and shoeprints to the mess. Another fellow, in a similar uniform as the assistant coroner's, walked up with black plastic bags draped over his arms.

Over the next hour, and two more margaritas, Sharon watched the most macabre dance one could imagine as they slid the bags up the length of the bodies, cut the cords, and carried the bodies across the sand to the step-van. At least they wore rubber gloves. The stench hung along the beach into the dark of night, even after the bodies and the head had been placed in the van. An attempt was made to take fingerprints before the bodies were bagged, and they swept the debris on the floor into small bags; by now, it would be like trying to solve a Chinese puzzle, blindfolded.

"Señorita, they are serving your dorado in the restaurant, would you like a piece?" Jose offered, when he brought her fourth margarita to her. "It is very good; the chef put cilantro butter on it as he sautéed the fish. It makes a great taco."

Suddenly famished, the tequilas had hid the fact that she hadn't eaten for almost eight hours and the fish tacos sounded like heaven. "Jose, bring me three, okay?"

"Si, Señorita. Tres tacos. Beans and rice?"

"No, Jose, just the tacos with guacamole, and let's change the margaritas to Bohemia, si?"

"*Bueno, dos Bohemia cerveza.*" Jose left for the kitchen.

Chapter 3

O'Mara sat in her makeshift camp and watched the inspector and his crew destroy a very interesting crime scene. Her four green margarita glasses sat in a neat row, lit by the light from the bar and the police van. The bodies had not left for San Jose; they were still stacked in the back of the coroner's van. She continued to stare at the box and the various numbers and codes written all over it. She knew the Pacific Container Line was a big operation; almost every time she went to the farmer's market in San Francisco she saw one of their ships heading into, or out of, Oakland, big red boats the same color as this container, containers all stacked with its brothers, fifteen-high.

Her watch said 9:03. Kevin should be back from his mother's. She wondered if he was home.

Technology, like everything else, could not hide even in this faraway part of the world. It came here because this quiet land didn't have cell phones and TV and soccer 24/7. Vacationers needed their phones, and so, as not to miss a beat or a peso, one of the world's richest men (who happened to be Mexican), and owner of the cellular phone market south of the United States, made sure that he would not lose one dollar the American tourists had to spend to stay connected to friends and families in the States and built the only cell phone system in Baja; the rates were usurious. Sharon clicked her cell on, watched it power up and find a signal. She punched in Kevin Bryan's number and was pleasantly surprised to hear it ring, and more shocked to have it answered.

"I was wondering how long it would be before you missed me, Sharon, my dear," Kevin answered, not even saying hello.

"Not long enough, I think," Sharon said.

Bryan had been a detective with the Lafayette police department for almost ten years, joining the East Bay city's police force after a tough time in Oakland. He had known Sharon almost as long. Close friends, almost to the point of being intimate, but never more than a brother-sister thing in their personal relationship. She was spending time in Mexico because she was not dead, all due to Kevin's timely arrival and shooting of the crazed transsexual that wanted to kill her.

"Unkind. Besides, I have your boyfriend sitting next to me, slobbering all over the end of my couch. Got him this afternoon. I missed your company and he is the next best thing."

"How's Basil?" she asked.

"Hungry. Guess they don't feed him much, like it was a Weight Watchers clinic for dogs. Since I got him home, he has eaten most of a bag of dog food."

"Don't let him eat too much or you won't be able to stay in the same room with him. Thanks. Got a story to tell you," Sharon said.

Sharon went through the whole day, fish, container, and Lopez-Peron. When she got to the box, he offered a comment.

"When I worked in Oakland, I had a few dealings with the container companies and their cargos, especially when the drug guys thought they could import the stuff hidden in the boxes. They were smart in some ways and dumb in others. Like the SKU number on a can of soup—every box has an identification code that tells where it has been, where it's going, and what's inside. We followed a couple of these back through a labyrinth of intentionally confusing routes and red herrings, all trying to tell us the box was different than what we found inside. But we were able to track most of them. A few were so well done that we never found the source and their point of origin. I think we might be able to track your box back. By the way, the newest way is to attach an RFID tag to the box so it can be scanned with a remote reader; it's a radio frequency ID tag, easier than trying to read a SKU, and only those with a receiver can ID the box. Get me the RFID tag and I can get you all the information you need. It's a lot like the *FasTrak* for the bridges; it gives the information to the scanner and then the computer knows who you are and deducts your money."

"Where is it?" Sharon asked.

"Usually near the end with the doors, on one side, high up. It's a small box. If you can get it, then we can get most of the information we need, and that's assuming the data is correct and not faked. These guys wanted this box to get where it was sent, to deliver a message, to make their point."

"I'll check with Lopez and see if he has a clue about getting the information off the tag; I'll let you know. Get a good night's sleep and give Basil a big kiss for me. Good night."

"Good night. Be careful, love ya."

3b

"Inspector Detective Lopez, when will you be returning to San Jose?" Sharon asked.

He'd watched her every step as she crossed the sand to the step-van, near the container; his eyes smiled. With every step and bounce she made, the small cigar left a halo of haze around his head. The phone never left his ear.

"Good evening, Señorita O'Mara, enjoying the show?" he asked, still attached to his phone.

"Interesting. Your crime scene is so messed up that not even the few geniuses working for you could straighten it out."

Clearly never one to take criticism well, especially from a woman, Lopez lashed out. "If it weren't for you and those fucking boat-jockeys, none of this would be here; I would not be here, and you would not be here eating tacos. Now I have to deal with all this shit and I don't need your amateurish comments to remind me of my job."

Letting his venting pass, Sharon asked, "Do you know if that box has an RFID unit on it? Might help."

"RDIF unit, que?"

"RFID tag, radio frequency identification; it`s a small box that sends out information on the container—where it's been, where it's going, and what's inside," Sharon said. "Did you get it yet?"

Quieting down a bit, Lopez looked at the container. "Where is it and how big is it?"

"High on the outside, away from prying hands and fingers, and safe from being knocked off."

The illuminated container stood like a ghostly red casket on a ramp ready to be commended to the deep. Only the soft sizzle of the waves rolling up the beach broke the silence. The inspector pulled his flashlight out of his pocket and played the light across the face of the box; Sharon followed the disk. On the side away from the hotel, they spied a dark gray cigarette-sized package secured to the box just below its top rail. It fit between two of the corrugated panels, out of harm's way when stacked next to another container.

Sharon pointed. "There, Inspector Lopez, I believe that's it."

"And what good is it to me?" His phone began emitting a strange sound, like Mexican trumpets mixed with salsa.

"*Si. Si, Imbycil, estupido. Si. Si, mayana.*" He turned to Sharon. "The driver with the flatbed can't be here until midday tomorrow. Now I will have to stay here tonight. The hotel will put me up; that's the least they can do for all of this bullshit. I'll pull the RFD thing off the container and have it checked at the port; as you said, maybe we can find out where it came from, maybe. The box can stay here till tomorrow. After it gets to San Jose, my men will go over it and see what they can find."

O'Mara's curiosity got the better of her. "I would be very interested in what you find out, Inspector Lopez."

"You would, why? You have nothing to do with this matter; it doesn't concern you."

"My gut wants to know. I'm a detective up in San Francisco and my gut tells me that this is something pretty big; do you know what's in the cardboard cartons in the container?"

"No, most of them are not marked. Some have what looks like Chinese characters stamped on them. It's not going anywhere and, now that the coroner has left and the bodies are on their way to San Jose, it can wait till tomorrow." He smiled and lit another of his small cigars; he lit her Marlboro.

Lopez propped a small ladder from the van against the side of the container. Shining the flashlight on the RFID, he asked one of his guards to get a chisel and hammer from the toolbox. Five minutes later, surprising Sharon by not hurting himself with the unfamiliar tools, the small package popped from the case, bounced off his forehead, and fell on the sand. Sharon, after the day she had had, thought it was a perfect ending. Lopez retrieved the box and held it up like a freshly caught trout; blood trickled down his forehead from the cut the unit had made during its attempted escape.

One of the guards handed Lopez a towel and pointed to his forehead. Lopez touched his cheek, saw the blood, and immediately put the towel against his face. The guard smiled and winked, as he passed by Sharon.

"You alright?"

"Si, Señorita, it's just a scratch, it's nothing." Sharon thought, *Then why are you acting like such a baby? Hell, Jesus, on the boat this morning, had a two-inch gash in his forehead, yet he went swimming after this damn thing.* A movement caught her eye near the front of the container; all the police, including Lopez, had their backs to the box. Sharon watched as two young boys carefully climbed on the ramp and slowly opened one of the doors (those fools had not even locked the doors); one went inside and passed out two cardboard cartons to his partner, who passed them down to a third boy hidden behind the ramp. The boys climbed down and, running as fast as they could, disappeared into the black of night. She smiled. "What the hell, everyone deserves a taste."

"You find this amusing, Miss O'Mara?" Lopez said, switching to English.

"Oh, no. It has been a strange day and I was just thinking about what's in that damn container. Hope it's worth all the trouble and death. Tell you what, if I buy you a drink and dinner, would you allow me to go to San Jose with you in the morning to see what that RFID says? I'm leaving tomorrow and, anyway, I need a ride, and it would be my honor to have dinner with you." She made every effort to be as civil as possible, even though the thought of dinner and his expected advances were more than she normally would endure. Maybe she could pry a bit more information out of him before she went home.

Lopez thought for moment, more than likely plotting his evening's hopeful debauchery, before he answered. "Señorita O'Mara, dinner with you would be an honor; let me get cleaned up and get my men situated here. I will meet you in an hour at the bar?"

3c

After a long shower, she dried her hair, slipped on a green silk shirt over a black bra and jeans, brushed on a faint touch of makeup to knock back her red cheeks (the sun had done its work), and strolled into the dining room. Inspector Lopez looked fresher, somehow; the cut on his forehead sported a small Band-Aid, the few blood spots on his uniform now gone. Sharon did her best to try and convince him of her sincerity as she walked across the dining room, almost every guy following her passage like she was Cleopatra entering Thebes, until they saw her destination; then they quickly went back to their drinks and dinner.

"Fabulous, simply fabulous. Please." Lopez stood and helped Sharon to her seat.

"Gracias, Inspector."

"Only English, Miss O'Mara. May I call you Sharon?" he asked, and didn't wait for an answer. "I'm off to a police conference on drugs, paid for by your government, in a week. It is in Houston and the practice will do me good. We are lucky here—drugs are less of a problem than on the mainland. I have a small force, but it's harder to hide here, unlike the bigger cities where the cartels just disappear into the masses of people. But they are coming, mostly because of the rich Americans who buy the coke and other things they want. All the vices are growing here because of the American dollar, so I get an American-paid vacation. Is not your country great?"

Yes, Inspector, just wonderful, she thought. *You're no different than some cops I know in the States, even a couple from my own unit after they came back from Iraq; they turned out to be no different than you.*

"Drinks?" a familiar voice said from behind Sharon.

"Buenos noches, Jose. Si, Johnny Walker Black, rocks. Señor Lopez?"

The inspector clearly had spent little time with strong women and was taken aback by her direct style. He looked at her; a slight wash of indignation flushed his cheeks. "I will have the same. "

The fish tacos seemed like hours ago and Sharon's hunger increased after the first scotch; Lopez's interest in her continued to grow, especially after his stories of crime-solving bravery and chasing bandits. He tried to pry out information about her detective work and why she came to this part of Mexico. "Just for the fishing and to get away from all the mundane work in San Francisco, just the fishing, the beach, and the food." The way he continued to look at her, she wasn't sure he heard anything she said. She could see his mind spin, hoping to find a way to get her to come to his room, or him to hers, for that matter. The three scotches didn't seem to lessen his ardor, but the two tequila shooters started to add up. She demurred.

* * *

Imagine forty-five million years ago: Vancouver sat due east of the current town of La Paz and, in another fifteen million years, Puerta Vallarta will sit where Mazatlan does today. Now, also imagine at the bottom of the abyss that forms the deep spine of the Sea of Cortez, there is a fissure that extends north to where Vancouver now sits. This crack splits the Sea of Cortez, bellies out in the Salton Sea, wiggles and waggles through California ranchland and vineyards, dives into the Pacific off the coast of San Francisco, then near Fort Ross, comes ashore like a tourist with a bad attitude, and eventually joins its annoying sisters as it moves north toward Alaska. She is one evil bitch, this crack in the world.

Sharon traced circles in the condensation on her glass, bored out of her mind and trying to keep her ride without having to leave the dining room with this buffoon. Their incredible dinner included yellowfin tuna, pargo, and her dorado; bowls of rice and the best refried beans she had ever eaten filled out the menu. She was sure it was the lard but didn't want to think of it. She started to say something in an effort to shut the man up when she noticed the saltshaker had begun to hula across the table and the silverware and her freshly filled glass of French chardonnay started to shake and rattle. Quickly joining the party, the dining room, and the rock it sat on began to do the shimmy; dance fever had set in.

"Fuck, earthquake," was all she could say before Inspector Lopez stood upright and extended his hand.

"I think, Sharon, we should go to the deck—now!"

The room shook for another five seconds and then suddenly stopped; the non-natives and non-Californians looked like they were about to pee in their pants.

"Just a mild one, señors and señoritas, she was not a big one," Mr. Valdez announced, as he made the rounds through the room assuring the guests of the situation. He passed Lopez and Sharon returning from the patio deck.

"Mas tequila," he said to Jose, trying to cover his concern. "That was not such a big one, si?" he said to Sharon.

"Not like some I have been through, but they all increase your anxiety; it's just where we live."

Señor Valdez's scratchy voice came over the intercom; a noticeable hum filled the space between his words, the system obviously underused.

"Good evening, excellent guests. For those who don't know it, that was one of our famous earthquakes. There have been others much longer and stronger, but this hotel is built on solid rock and is safely placed high above the water. Many have asked if there is a chance of a tsunami. We sincerely hope not. This fault in the Sea of Cortez, she seldom causes this. There is no damage to the hotel and the bar is safe and open for business. Thank you." A moment passed and the room offered a collective exhalation, like all the guests had been holding their breaths; loud orders to the bar could be heard.

"Now, where were we, Señorita?" Lopez asked, dabbing the napkin on his forehead. A touch of red showed where he patted the Band-Aid. Sharon only shook her head at the all-out effort of this man.

The speakers crackled again and a louder and more panicked voice overpowered Lopez's question. "Ladies and gentlemen, I have been informed by the authorities that there may be a slight possibility of a tsunami hitting the beach here in maybe fifteen minutes. A boat about fifty miles out in the ocean noticed a large swell heading west. The Coast Guard informs us to keep to high ground. We are over forty feet above the ocean here, so please remain calm, and don't go down to the beach. We are asking everyone along the beach to move up to the road and to get well above the sea. We had a small tsunami a few years ago and it only washed up the beach and then back out—no one was killed or injured. Please remain calm. I will keep you informed and will make announcements when I hear anything new."

Concern returned to Lopez's face; Sharon wondered how this man had made it so far in the local police department. Lopez downed another drink and walked out to the patio, joining maybe fifty guests that stood with a drink in one hand, cigarettes and cigars in the other. All watched the black sea; the moon, almost full, cast a long, fractured beam of light across the ruffled surface of the ocean. He lit Sharon's Marlboro and then one of his own cigars, this one longer and more important than the others. "Cubana," he offered.

"There, I saw something," one guest yelled, near the patio's railing. A murmur passed through the crowd. Sharon looked down to the beach. A lone jeep, its headlights bouncing on the sand, headed toward them, its siren blare cutting through the silence on the patio, clearing the beach. The red shipping container, still dimly lit by the hotel's floodlights, sat alone on the ramp. The police van was gone. She watched the jeep pull up the steep road cut into the side of the cliff and head to the highway.

She looked back at the beach; it seemed wider than a minute ago; the floodlights no longer illuminated the surf line; it had disappeared. She only saw sand. The boat ramp extended down the sandy shingle and its end was visible; the surf line had disappeared into the dark. A sloshing sound, as if a thousand people were crying "shhhhhh," came from the blackness of the ocean.

A woman screamed, "My God, we're all dead." Her panic now inhabited every guest and patron in the room; it sat at the bar and offered drinks to everyone; it was his party. Panic leered at everyone, raising its bony hand in salute.

The surf rolled furiously back onto the beach, pushing boats and busted mooring lines with it; Sharon watched two cruisers roll and flood before they were smashed against the cliff. The surf tumbled, as if an angry storm had settled off the coast throwing everything it could find against the land. But there was no wind, no noise, no driving rain, only panic having another drink at the bar. Terrified voices filled the air. Sharon ignored the screams from the terrace; the tsunami's tumult was thirty feet below her. She had watched hurricanes kick up higher and angrier waves at this same resort.

"This is nothing," she said out loud to no one in particular.

"Que?" Lopez said.

"Nothing, Inspector, nothing. But I do suggest you watch your container," she said, pointing down to the beach.

The red PCL container, still chained to the winch high up the beach, twisted and rolled in the surf, desperately trying to escape its tenuous attachment and get back to the sea. A smaller yet still powerful second surge pushed the box higher and, as it returned to the ocean, ripped the chain and the winch from its mooring and pulled the box into the blackness; the winch bounced and disappeared in the surf. Sharon thought she saw it briefly drift through the moon's long glare, a dark box bobbing on the now softening sea. Then she remembered that the kids had not shut the door after their burglary.

Chapter 4

Like most mornings on the East Cape, the sun rises quickly out of the sea and a salty dampness hangs about the Hotel Buena Ventura. It's easy to slide your finger across the glass tabletops and leave a damp cleansing streak. Experience and time have moved the casitas out of the reach of the ocean during its angry hurricane seasons. Nothing had been destroyed or damaged and not one rental car had been lost above the surge line. The beach was, on the other hand, a disaster: two cruisers were crushed and lying at the base of the cliff, the hotel's umbrellas could not be found, plastic coolers lay strewn about like dice on a gritty bar, and unidentified debris littered the sand as far as you could see. Luckily, no one died. At breakfast, Señor Valdez told everyone there would be no fishing today; they were looking for three boats that broke from their moorings. Fishing would be rescheduled among the remaining boats. Sharon could see Gregorio's boat still safely moored within the makeshift harbor.

"Señorita O'Mara, I apologize. I will not be able to take you to San Jose and the airport; the Army has me going north to help with some recovery problems. The tsunami washed much further inland up there, and there're people missing," Lopez said, sounding disappointed. Sharon was not.

"I understand; I will take the hotel bus. Many are leaving today and the missing boats complicate the fishing. We were lucky, si?"

"Si, very lucky. I will not waste time trying to find that damn container; I'm sure it's on the bottom of the sea. We will process the bodies, but the coroner says there is no identification on any of them; maybe he can get fingerprints. That will only help if they're in the system, maybe INTERPOL, assuming we can even figure out where they came from. I will have that radio thing checked; maybe that'll help."

"RFID. Can you send me any information that you find on the container? I'm just curious, that's all. If you find out who the men were, and where they came from, I would also be interested," Sharon said.

"Curious? You have nothing to do with this. Why do you really want to know, or even care?"

"I don't know, but I have a nagging sense about this whole thing. Besides, it was the biggest catch I made during this whole trip and I'll hang a picture of the container next to my marlin." She smiled at Lopez, using her "I'm just a girl and you're so strong" look. He fell for it.

"You're like other women I know, always saying things I don't understand. Yes, Miss O'Mara, I will send you the information. Where shall I send it to?"

Sharon handed him her card. "Email or fax, I should be home tonight and I look forward to the information—maybe tomorrow or the next day?"

"I'll see. I'm not sure when I'll get back to San Jose, but, Señorita, thank you for last evening and the pleasure of your company. I will make sure you get the information. Gracias, and I hope to see you soon, si?"

"Time will tell, Inspector Lopez, time will tell."

Sharon confirmed her two o'clock flight back to Oakland. After a quick conversation with Kevin about when to pick her up, she calculated that she would be home and in bed by ten.

The bus was scheduled to leave at eleven thirty for the two o'clock flight. Sharon filled a breakfast plate of fruit from the buffet and sat on the terrace overlooking the beach, when she saw Gregorio walking up the beach with a young boy. The youngster looked like one of the gang of container thieves. She caught Gregorio's eye, waved, and motioned that she would come down to the beach.

"Buenos dias, Gregorio."

"Good morning, Señorita, we were lucky. My boat, she still floats and the damn box from hell is gone. I'm not sorry. It was bad luck; we are lucky no one was hurt."

"Your house?" she asked.

"I'm up the hill, away from the sea. I know what she can do. So I keep my family up there." He pointed high above the road. "Besides, I can at least watch the sunrises more better from there, it's a good vista. This is my boy, Eduardo. This is Señorita O'Mara, she is my client."

The boy stuck his hand out and offered a tentative "Good morning."

"Good morning to you, Eduardo. You have grown a lot during the last year, and your English is getting better."

"Si, he is growing too fast. Señorita, my boy told me something last night I was not happy with and I'm not sure how to deal with it."

"Si?"

"Well, I know you were interested in the box and what was in it, not just the bodies." Gregorio crossed himself. "Well, the attraction of the box also affected my boy and two of his friends; they snuck into the box and stole two cartons. Now they're ashamed. Their friends, who dared them to do it, are now laughing at them. I think he has something you might like to see. *Eduardo, ir a buscar el cuadro de.*" The boy ran up the beach to Gregorio's pickup, retrieved a cardboard box, and returned.

"Señorita, please look inside; my son, while still a thief, is ashamed of what he stole."

Sharon folded back the top of the carton and pushed away the packing material and smiled. Orange and black leather peeked out between the wrapping papers. Straps and very shiny gold buckles flashed in the morning sun. A prominent oval label sat neatly stitched to the side. The label said: *STIA.*

Sharon smiled; no wonder the boys were being ridiculed, they stole handbags. She also wondered why four men were hanging in the container when all it may have contained were purses.

"Gregorio, I saw the boys steal the boxes, though technically they may still have been your boxes, but we will never know now. Did both boxes have handbags?"

"Si, his embarrassment could not be hidden. He showed me both; they were stuffed with purses, many colors and mostly two shapes, this one and another one. The boys don't know what to do with them; his sister has already claimed one. Should I tell the inspector?"

"I don't think Inspector Lopez cares anymore; the tidal wave changed the course of his investigation and he has other things to do. I would not bother him. I hope your boy has learned a lesson," Sharon said.

"Si, and so has his bottom. He will also go with me to the boat to wash it down, and help fix what needs fixing. He is a good boy; he and his friends are all learning. Are these valuable?"

"Gregorio, see that name there, it says *STIA*. It's an Italian firm that makes the most expensive handbags in the world; these bags may be worth eight thousand American dollars, each. But I would not try to sell these to the tourists; there may be too many questions. Let the ladies and the children use them. Have fun."

Gregorio stood, stunned. Each of these bits of leather sold for more than he made some summers when the fishing was bad and the fuel cost was high. The other box at home had ten bags and was worth eighty thousand dollars; he could retire on that, no more goddamn fishing and stupid American tourists. Freedom.

"Don't go there, Gregorio," Sharon cautioned, seeing his face. "You cannot sell them, and if you do, the Federalies will take a very close look at where you got them from and why you are selling them. Besides, did you not tell your son that he should not be a thief? And now you're thinking like one. Be very careful."

"Si, you're right," he said, after thinking her comment through. "Yes, that's exactly what would happen." He didn't want any trouble and told Sharon about his cousin who tried to sell some grass to a tourist and was now in a Mazatlán jail for two more years.

"Please, you take two, any two you want," he said. "I will

drop the rest in the sea where they belong; I will do it later to-day—get rid of these cursed things. But you paid for the boat so please take them, something to remember us by. You have always been good to me and my family, so please."

Sharon O'Mara hesitated. What would she do with an eight-thousand-dollar handbag? She had nothing to go with it. But what the hell. Gregorio certainly expected her to take them and she also hoped he would dump the rest; they would only bring trouble on him if he tried to sell them, even if he got a hundred dollars apiece from a knowledgeable tourist in Cabo. He was too naïve to pull it off without trouble. "I will only if you promise me that you'll dump the rest at sea; let the niña keep hers, but never tell her what they are worth, okay?"

"Si, I will. I had a weak moment, but you're right. I will explain it all to the boy. He will be disappointed, but I will leave out what they are worth; he will understand. We are simple people here. We see much of the outside world with all the touristas and their things; the children think about the outside world and they will learn and make choices. I can only try to help."

"You are a good father and a good man; they will grow up and make you proud."

He pointed to the cardboard box, and smiled. "Choose, Señorita. I like the orange one and the dark green one, but what do I know."

"Good choices, I will take those two." She picked out the orange one and laid it alongside her leg, admiring the look and feel. She suddenly laughed at her pose and the surroundings; it was weird to do this in a store in San Francisco and even stranger to do this on a debris-covered beach in Cabo. *Oh, the burden we women carry.*

She decided to carry the orange bag and put the dark green version in her suitcase. She had never been stopped by Customs coming or going to Mexico, and with the handbag on her arm, it would be even less of a problem. It took another hour to pack her reels and gear and stow the rods in their hard six-foot-long case. She never hauled fish back to the States like the tourists.

She did it once years ago, but when she opened the cooler she found that the hotel had frozen all the meat into one large thirty-pound block of flesh so she vowed never to do that again. "Eat them or release them" was her motto now.

4b

The trip to the airport and the flight home was uneventful, except, while going through the quasi-security at the airport, a blonde, lanky, twenty-something fashionista kept staring at her handbag. Of all the hundreds milling about in the terminal, only one recognized the handbag and the label; good, it was less trouble than she thought.

The bags and gear just fit in Kevin's ten-year-old Corolla; the rod case stuck out the rear window, and a bungee cord held the trunk closed.

"You travel with more crap than anyone I know, Sharon O'Mara. No one goes to Mexico with this much stuff. I need only a pair of shorts and a Hawaiian shirt," Kevin said, as they headed up Highway 24 to the Caldecott Tunnel.

"And that's why, after a week, no one wants to sit next to you at dinner. I have to have this much stuff; a girl must be prepared. Basil alright?"

"He is great and misses you; he seems to know when you're on your way home, he's all excited. Are you okay? The news had a few short clips on the earthquake and tsunami. Other than a few people missing near a small town north of the Cape, it didn't seem to be a big deal. After that Indonesian tsunami, the press was all over this. Did you find out more about the box?"

"It's gone; the surge came in and took it. After they removed the bodies, they were waiting for a tow truck to move it to San Jose. Before they could load it, the earthquake hit and all the evidence, such as it was, floated out to sea and sunk. Some boys were playing in it, that's another story, left the door open, and away it went. Inspector Detective Lopez decided not to try and find it, probably his best decision. Anyway, as they say, all I got when I went to Mexico was a tee shirt and this very expensive handbag. Like the color? I have another in the suitcase."

Kevin looked at the orange bag and smiled. "Why did you buy that? They have purses up here."

"Purses; good God, man, don't you know anything? They're called handbags, and for what this one is worth, they should be called goddamn gold-plated, dipped-in-yogurt-and-honey handbags."

"A handbag, a purse, bag, sack, what's the difference? Never could figure out the attachment women have for those things, and don't get me started on shoes; at least you're not over the top there. Anyway, back to my point, why did you buy one down there?"

"Didn't buy it; it was a gift from a very nice young thief who stole it from the container just before the tsunami dragged the damn thing out to its burial at sea. His dad, Gregorio, you remember him, the boat captain, had his son march up and apologize for stealing the bags. Little did either of them know that they're worth thousands of dollars, each."

"What? A damn purse for thousands of dollars? Good Lord."

"Handbag! Maybe eight thousand for this one, though it's not one I've seen before, so who knows? Anyway, I told them to get rid of the rest of the bags. It would only cause them trouble if the word got out; hopefully, he deep-sixed the rest, maybe fifteen bags. My guess is that the cartons in the shipping container held handbags and other such things. No way to confirm it, but it's very strange that four dead men were strung up as examples to whomever these handbags were going to. After I get settled, I think I will visit the STIA store in Union Square to get an idea of its worth and see what else just might be going on. Hungry? I'm famished."

They stopped at a spaghetti house in Lafayette, stuck between a gas station and a strip mall, picked up two Styrofoam boxes of takeout, spent three minutes calming Basil down at Kevin's house, squeezed him under the rod case in the back seat, kept pushing back his nose out of the front seat where the takeout was, and, at 8:10, finally pulled up to Sharon's bungalow in

Walnut Creek.

"Made it; I will be in bed by ten."

"What? An offer!" Kevin said, with a laugh.

"The only dreams fulfilled tonight will be mine and in my own bed."

She dumped her gear in the living room, threw the suitcase in the corner, opened a rich sangiovese, cut thick slices of olive bread, and laid two heaping plates of pasta on the dining room table.

"Missed you. Did you get a chance to relax between bouts of murdering fish?"

"Slept like a log with no aftereffects from that Clayburn thing; in fact, for three days it never even flashed in my head. I love it there; we need to go back some time. Gregorio and Jesus said that they missed the tall Irish gringo and wanted to make sure to say hola. They are all well, and the little one, Eduardo, isn't so little and learned a lesson about being a thief. His father won't let that happen again."

Basil nudged Sharon's hip and set his sloppy face on her lap; she scratched between his eyes, watched them glaze over, and, after a turn around the table and a slow revolution in an ever tightening circle, he lay next to her with a noticeable sigh. Sharon regaled Kevin with fish stories and how things had changed, some for the better, and some for the worse.

"Mostly sad," she said. "That simple point of land has become the poster child for tourists and cruise ships; it's a far cry from the dirt streets that used to be Cabo San Lucas. Air-conditioning and golf courses have changed it all. The lives of the people are better and worse."

Sharon took a quick shower after Kevin left, crawled into bed, and, in two minutes, fell asleep. Basil slept in the doorway and kept guard. The clock said 10:14.

4c

The next morning, Sharon stowed her gear in the garage attic after a thorough cleaning, drying, and greasing of all the rods and reels and did the same for the lures, leaders, and plugs. She ran the clothes through the washer and dryer and by ten thirty, when the cell phone rang, all evidence of Mexico was gone.

"Señorita O'Mara, this is Inspector Detective Lopez, you had a safe trip home, si?"

"Inspector, yes I did, thank you, and thank you for the very interesting evening; you certainly know how to entertain a girl."

The sarcasm seemed lost on Lopez. "I have some news about the radio tag on the box. I will email it to you, okay?"

"Email, you have email?"

"Please, Sharon, yes, I have email. I will copy the information and send it to the address on your card, maybe later today. It doesn't make much sense to me, but maybe you can make something of it. The bodies are all oriental, maybe Chinese, no identification. There were exploded bullet fragments in their skulls, probably small caliber. If there is more, I will pass on the datos, data, when I get it." Lopez's phone began to break up. "I'm leaving San Jose and I will lose the signal, adios."

Sharon stood in the kitchen, the cell phone against her ear, with nothing exciting to do until the emails arrived. After a stop at the post office to retrieve her mail, and at Starbucks for a venti black, she curled up with Basil on the floor of the cottage. The mail filled the plastic postal carton to the top and in ten minutes a pile of catalogs and other debris sat to one side. The real mail, such as it was, sat in a much smaller pile on the right. The usual bills and bank statements would hold until she found the courage to look at them. There were six from her medical insurer and four from the hospital. She still had the glow of Mexico and they could wait. They would only be asking for more money, money she didn't have. Basil stretched out his long frame and pushed over the pile of catalogs; smiling, she restacked them and threw them in the recycle bin. One line of type caught her eye as it tumbled into the bin, an ad card for Mediterranean cruises. In fine print, it said: "Owned and operated by Pacific Container Line."

"PCL, what do you know, buddy?" Basil's ears picked up. "My old friends from Mexico. Why don't we chase them down a bit?"

After two hours on the internet, Sharon learned more about the shipping company and container freight than her brain could hold. PCL was huge. They had over fifty container ships worldwide, ten cruise ships in every major tourist market, and it moved over two million boxes a year. She easily understood how someone could ship one box full of death and handbags and have it slip through unnoticed. She also saw images of container ships with damaged sterns and boxes hanging over their sides, and others dangling and missing from the interlocking stacks. She could only guess at the real number of lost containers and goods. When she was younger, she had ridden out storms on freighters and understood completely what the ocean could do to a ship, let alone one stacked a hundred and thirty feet high with thousands of boxes. What amazed her even more was that there were boats that could carry up to fifteen thousand containers at a time, boxes full to bursting with food, toys, cars, clothing, machinery, liquor, and even handbags. The commerce of the world and the underworld moved innocently from port to port unseen by everyone, and only a small plastic box stuck to the top of the container helped them to be separated from each other and get them to their destinations. The destination was what was important, not necessarily the contents, and that could be falsified and only verified if opened. And it seemed that the only thing Homeland Security focused on was radiation, with their scanners and X-rays; everything else could be hidden. And what real threat would a few hundred handbags pose?

According to the shipping schedule on their website, a PCL ship made port in Oakland twice a week, usually Mondays and Thursdays, and it looked like there were at least eight of their largest ships in a continuous circuit around the Pacific: China, Mexico, Long Beach, Oakland, Tacoma, Korea, and back to China. Other PCL boats hit at least twenty other cities on different circuits that included Japan and Vancouver. Any boat moving along the western Mexican coast would pass the Baja Peninsula and, under the right conditions, lose containers; there were hundreds of opportunities. With the right information from Lopez, maybe she could work backward and track the ship back to its last stop in China; it all depended on the four bodies from the container. Even if dead and rotting, they could tell a good coroner how long they had been deceased, maybe what they had for their last meals, maybe even things indigenous to where they once lived. The findings hinged on the competency of the "cruise" ship coroner and his assistant.

Sharon received Lopez's email late in the afternoon; a PDF of a scanned printout was attached. The manifest told the story of the box. It started in the Port of Chiwan, Guangdong, China, and was to be delivered to the Port of Oakland. It left China three weeks before the bodies were found and was going to arrive in Oakland just last week. The container was loaded on the *Duncan Dynasty*; she remembered all the PCL boats had the suffix *"Dynasty,"* and it was container number two in a shipment of three boxes. A quick check on Google Earth showed that the port was north of the harbor from Hong Kong and part of a huge port complex that served this southern region of China.

Sharon sent an email back to Lopez thanking him for the information. She also took the opportunity to ask him for a copy of the coroner's reports on each of the bodies, especially his estimates about when they died, abnormal body conditions, and what they ate last. Maybe she could piece something together.

Basil stood, looked at the door, and barked deeply and softly three times just before the doorbell rang.

"He's a better and more intimidating doorbell," Kevin said, as he kissed her on the cheek. "Must have known it was me; I've been here when he told a bell ringer what he really thought."

"Good boy. Next time grab his leg and hold tight," Sharon ordered. "Why the honor of your presence, Officer?"

"It's social and business. First, I wanted to see how you were doing since your cell phone must be dead. Doing very well, I see," Kevin said, checking her out. "And, second, I have made an appointment for you tomorrow at the Port of Oakland to meet with Thaddeus Spinos to talk to him about your container. He is very interested in the farm tools that were lost overboard; they were what was supposed to have been in your container."

"Damn, I completely forgot to charge the thing since I got back. One second." Sharon walked down the short hall and returned with her phone and plugged it into the charger. "Port of Oakland. Did you say anything about the handbags?"

"No, Spinos is a fellow who was recommended to me by one of my old contacts at the port; he says Spinos is a straight shooter and knows more about the business than anyone on the docks. I gave him a call and he said he would be glad to talk to you about shipping, containers, RFIDs, and where the box may have come from. I made an appointment at four thirty. Only one ship has lost containers in the last few months; it was the PCL ship *Duncan Dynasty*."

"My appointment secretary strikes again, thanks. That was the ship listed as the carrier, according to the printout that Lopez sent me. It'll give me some time to go into San Francisco to the STIA store to get an idea about my bag, maybe ask a few questions, and hopefully hear no lies."

Chapter 5

Since the Doris Morgan thing, Sharon hadn't owned a car. After the police scraped up what was left of her old Jaguar, and thanks to Bryan's insistence that it was a part of the investigation, she didn't have to pay for its removal and cleanup. Getting around had not been a problem since leaving the hospital; she had nowhere to go. The insurance paid for a few nights in Mexico, but now that money was gone. The Walnut Creek Bay Area Rapid Transit (BART) station, two blocks away, gave her good access to Oakland, San Francisco, the airport, and the world; only she still didn't have anywhere to go. It was the small trips that were trouble, and they required a rental car. Basil's world had also shrunk to the backyard and neighborhood walks; she could tell he missed his walks in the dog park.

The STIA store was an easy commute: a half block from Union Square, two blocks from the Powell Street station, and two blocks from one of her favorite Italian restaurants; she would make a day of it. Kevin offered to pick her up at the West Oakland station for the Port of Oakland meeting; she demurred.

"There's no reason for you to get involved with this," she said. "You have enough on your plate right now, especially with that double murder rich guy case; I'm just checking on a few things. Thanks for setting up the meeting; I will tell Spinos that you said hello."

He sounded hurt, but it was Kevin's normal Irish feelings coming out. He wanted to be involved; she just wanted him at arm's length, at least for now. He wanted to help, but she wanted to keep their friendship affable. She would take a taxi to the port office at Jack London Square.

The STIA store sat nestled, like a small leather-bound book with gilt letters, between two huge tomes of glass and stainless steel. The gold letters, on the storefront window glass, announced the name of the store and stood larger than the shop's front door. The thick glass shielded the displays of handbags from the sun. Three bags sat encased in smaller glass cubes, as if they were expensive museum pieces; lookee-no-touchee, was what was really being said.

Sharon reset the green bag over her shoulder and walked through the door into an invisible fog of deep rich leather (she flashed on saddle shops from her youth), inhaled deeply, and shook her head to clear both the memory and the fragrance. A soft chime echoed in the tall, narrow space.

"Good morning, may I help you?" a sharp-nosed young woman, oriental, Chinese, maybe thirty, asked, with a slight Italian accent. It was all disconcerting, to say the least. Her hair, black with a shard of rose pink that slashed across her head to end behind her right ear, capped a round face framed between golden disk earrings that almost hung to her shoulders. Black seemed to be her favorite color, except for the pink exclamation. Her eyes scanned Sharon professionally from head to toe, and dilated when they caught sight of the handbag under her arm. Her face blossomed with a smile that exposed her brilliant teeth, as if she were a lioness spotting her first warm meal in a week. She quickly moved from around the counter into the store.

"Yes, yes, may I help you with anything?" she offered without breaking her grin. She tried hard not to look at Sharon's handbag; it was difficult.

"No. Just looking."

The clerk tried to cover her disappointment, but gave Sharon room to move about the shop. She and the clerk were alone. The shelf, thick glass and steel, held an assortment of bags and clutches that surprised her; the colors were bolder than the usual fare in department stores, the stitching sharper and the hardware almost jewel-like. Impressed by what she saw, Sharon remembered that the last bag she bought cost one hundred and eighty dollars, all because it had an interior pocket large enough to quietly hold her Beretta. None of these would work even though both the pistol and the bag had been made in Italy. No prices hung on the bags; if you had to ask, you were in the wrong store. She turned to the clerk who had repositioned herself behind the glass case.

"Are you the manager?"

"No, madam, Ms. Luca is taking an early lunch. She should be back any time though. Is there something I can help with?" The Italian accent melted a bit into Southern California valley girl with a Chinese face.

"Ms. Luca, excellent. I will get a cup of coffee and be back in say—fifteen minutes."

Sharon turned and walked out the door, not even saying goodbye. She left the girl standing behind the glass box full of bags with more questions than answers. The handbag certainly left an impression; she didn't leave her business card. The girl would pass on a lot of information to Ms. Luca before she returned.

After a latte on the plaza at Union Square, Sharon walked the streets surrounding the remodeled square, not a bad job, she thought, even though the grass on the terraces was thin from all the wear. Twenty-two minutes later, she walked through the heavy glass door once again.

Two women stood at the case, Pinkie and a very elegantly dressed woman: black St. John knit, long glowing raven black hair, and just the right amount of jewelry to accent the suit. This woman knew how to dress.

Pinkie smiled, St. John stared at the handbag.

"You may go to lunch now, Ms. Lau," St. John said to Pinkie. A "May I help you?" flew sharply toward Sharon.

Sharon watched Pinkie quickly retrieve her cloth purse and scoot out the door, with only a brief look as she passed.

"Like it?" Sharon said, turning toward Ms. Luca fully exposing the handbag. Ms. Luca tapped her patent leather toe for a few seconds, looked at the bag, and then at her.

"Where?"

"Mexico."

"Impossible, no."

"Si. That's where I found it."

"Impossible, that bag will not be available until the fall."

"Nevertheless, I found it in Mexico."

"We have no stores in Mexico. The new store in Mexico City will not open until July, and Acapulco will follow in November. Mexico, impossible." She waved her hand, as if swatting at bugs.

Sharon walked about the store, admiring the bags on the shelves, making sure she touched most of them. The leather was the richest and softest she had ever felt.

"This bag, how much?" Sharon asked, holding up a deep tan handbag.

Ms. Luca, confused, looked at her, not wanting to let her get away without more information. "That particular handbag is five thousand eight hundred dollars. It is available in three colors; the other two colors have to be ordered. We don't carry them at this store. We can get the other colors overnight from our Rodeo Drive store. It will be delivered, by our own messenger, anywhere in the Bay Area, tomorrow afternoon."

"Thank you." O'Mara continued to look. Ms. Luca's impatience was tangible and her tapping was louder.

"Miss, let's cut through the crap; tell me exactly where you bought or acquired that bag, or should I call the police?"

Sharon smiled. "Finally, the response I was looking for. Yes, I do want to tell you about this bag, but I also want to know why you're so agitated about its presence in this shop. Your clerk damn near had a fit when I walked in. What's so important about this old bag?"

"That particular bag will not be released until the fall for the STIA winter collection, so it's hardly old. I, and maybe ten others within the company, have seen the real bags; only sketches have been released to store staff with some details left out. Your bag includes those details. You should not have that bag, yet . . ."

"Yet here it hangs, comfortable on my shoulder and quite luscious on my arm." Sharon was having too much fun. "When will your assistant be back?"

"When I call her on her cell phone. She knows that she has to leave for certain clients and stay away until I ask her to return. Let's just close the shop for a bit." Luca went to the door, placed a neatly printed sign in a slot on the door, and twisted the lock. "Now, miss, where the hell did you get that bag?"

A low coffin-shaped glass case extended out from the wall; seven handbags sat innocently inside. Sharon noted the glass looked strong enough so she boosted her fanny up on the case, sat on it, crossed her legs, and smiled.

"My name is Sharon O'Mara. I'm what might be called 'in salvage.'" She had rehearsed this presentation a hundred times in her head. "Yes, I did find this wonderful bag in Mexico. Let me tell you a story."

A half hour later, Ms. Luca stood speechless and, more than once, said she could not believe a word of it. Her protests fell to the side each time she looked at the bag; questions kept forming, yet were never asked.

"Let me be frank and open with you, Miss O'Mara, all our bags are made in southern France in a small, very secure atelier. It employs about one hundred craftsmen. The leathers travel a circuitous route through China and an Eastern European country before it reaches France. Our hardware is made in India with gold and silver plate accents. None of this is secret. Everyone in the high-end part of this industry uses many of the same shops and manufacturers, but they keep everything separate and very secure; one screw-up and they lose all the contracts. Only about thirty to forty bags are produced each day; we keep the supply very small and the demand very high."

"And your part in this is?" Sharon asked.

"My family owns the company, and my role is manager of this shop and the management and control of the market in the United States. I spend half my life on the road in New York and in Italy. We are headquartered in a wonderful old building in Florence just around the corner from the Uffizi Gallery. Our primary investor lives just outside of town; she wants to keep the business close. My father and brother run the company; Father controls the manufacturing and design, my brother, the sales and marketing. We don't have a star designer, just a very good staff of four that follows our lead. In reality, we are a small family company with a huge reputation. That's not unusual in this business, I assure you. May I look at the bag?"

Sharon handed the handbag to Ms. Luca. She looked out the window and saw a pink stripe of hair bounce past the last pane of glass. Luca's eyes followed Sharon's. "She is just an hourly clerk, been with me for about six months. I have two others that split the remaining shifts. All of our employees know nothing of the workings of the company. What's your take on this situation, Ms. O'Mara?" Ms. Luca hefted the bag and noticed its weight. Her eyes went to Sharon's face with a question in them.

"Please call me Sharon, and a girl needs all the protection she can carry these days. I think this bag was made in China, a fake or a knockoff. Something happened in China and they sent the message of four dead men to prove their sincerity. Whatever it is, the lives of four men meant far less than the money or value of the goods they were getting. Money, drugs, arms, terror, lots of things move about in the world and have suppliers and buyers. Sometimes goods are easier to launder than money."

"Thank you, Sharon, my name is Evelyn. Whoever made this bag did a very good job, none of the usual bad stitching and hardware, and the large interior pocket can accommodate all sorts of things." Evelyn felt the heft of the pistol in the side pocket. "The color is just a shade off but, since no one has seen the new bags, the color is close enough. You said there were two other containers?" She gently set the bag on the counter; a muffled tap announced the gun against glass.

"Yes, the manifest from the RFID said it was box two of three. I assume the others made it to the port in Oakland. The ship, the *Duncan Dynasty*, landed about a week ago, after a stop in Long Beach. I'm meeting with a fellow from the port later today, Thaddeus Spinos."

"I know him; we often fly our bags in from Italy and sometimes we have them shipped in containers. He seems to be a good guy; he has been very helpful. I knew him when I ran another shop here in the square; all our goods for that shop came by boat. You mentioned RFID; we use that system as well. We are one of the first companies to secure a small grain-sized ID tag inside the bag that gives all the particulars, such as when and where it was made; the buyer of the bag is added to the tag at the time of sale so that, if stolen, it can be identified later. To remove it, you have to severely damage the bag."

"Like an ID tag for dogs and cats?"

"Yes, wait just a minute." Evelyn walked to the counter and removed a small handheld device that looked similar to a TV remote. She passed it over the bag. "No tag, nothing. Let me show you what I mean." She passed the reader over a bag on the counter; data began to stream out on a small piece of paper. "See, the piece of paper shows this entire bag's particulars; your bag does not have one. Yes, it's a fake, but there are fakes and replicas all over the place. There will always be knockoffs and there is nothing I can do about it. We could spend a lot of money chasing them and we would only reduce our profits. They say copies are the sincerest form of flattery; bullshit. It's just plain theft. We watch what we can do, and when some of the other houses, the bigger ones like Louis Vuitton and Gucci, make a grand gesture, we go along for the ride, but not the cost. It's the price of being successful. Our RFID tag surprisingly helps with our cache of clientele as well. I've had women walk in with a bag just to have it scanned. One was shocked to learn that her daughter's bag was not as legit as she said; it was probably stolen and sold to the girl from the back of a truck. We stayed out of the fight, but the young lady was in trouble; I am sure of that. You said there was another bag from the same container."

"Yes, same style, a different color, burnt orange."

"That is interesting; we decided not to make that color this year, went with a plum. That means that whoever stole the information got it before the last meeting we had when we finalized the colors and the designs. That's very interesting. You said salvage; what do you mean?"

"I work to help retrieve lost goods, money, valuables, and even reputations. I work hourly and have all my expenses paid. I start with a sizable retainer and plan to have the account updated monthly with a specific amount of money. When the job is completed, and everyone is happy, leftover cash in the account is returned. I use a simple contract and I set up a separate account for each client. I also try to work with only one client at a time; it helps to keep my head straight."

Evelyn smiled. "You didn't come here to parade that thing about, did you?"

"No, ma'am, I did not. I thought there might be something that I could help you with, and after the last hour, I honestly believe there is. It's not only the fakes, but the distinct probability that someone is stealing your styles and designs, and there may even be more to this—there usually is with smuggling. Maybe they're passing on the information to one of your competitors; it is a rough racket even with high-quality goods, or so I have heard." She returned Evelyn Luca's smile.

Luca turned away and walked about the shop, straightening bags and setting them upright. After a minute, she looked at Sharon. "How about we do this? I will hire you to find out what you can and who is responsible for this, and we get them put in jail. I will put $15,000 in an account to get you started. What do you think?"

"You don't screw around, do you?" Sharon said. "What about this? I become your newest employee and that will provide me access to the warehouse and other places that I need to get into. This way, it doesn't look like I'm some official snooper asking questions and making people nervous."

"No, I don't screw around, especially when it comes to this company. I like the proposition; you can start Monday at three. I will give you training then about how to deal with customers; you will have a loose shift, allowing you to do whatever you need to do. Have you ever worked retail?"

"For about six months after I came back from Iraq. I worked at Macy's just around the corner; I needed a few dollars and that was the best available job at the time. The hours and the wages stunk."

"Iraq?"

"Army, military police, two tours."

"Fascinating," Luca said. "You are a woman with surprises and secrets. Working here won't be much different than there—Macy's, not Iraq—Sharon." She looked at the door with an impatient Pinkie standing at the threshold. Evelyn walked to the door and opened it. "Doris, meet our newest employee, Sharon O'Mara."

Sharon did a double take on the name. *Doris, damn, just what I need is another Doris,* she thought to herself.

5b

Sharon walked the three blocks to the Powell Street station, past panhandlers, bums, society gals, and more suits than she ever saw in Walnut Creek; it was the big city, after all. She got off at West Oakland. The station sits high above industrial and old residential developments, the view isn't bad, and, if it weren't for the fear of leaving the platform and walking to your car, it's okay. The cabs queued under the station; the ride to Jack London Square took five minutes.

Security at the port office was tight. The guard asked for ID, showed her where to sign in, handed her a tag, and told her to put it on. Thaddeus Spinos, who was cordial, had black curly hair, broad shoulders, a tight gut, and was good looking, met her in the hall outside his office.

"How's Bryan? Have not seen him in a while, worked on a couple of problems we had here at the port when he was with Oakland, good guy. He never said a thing about you during all those years; I'm disappointed. Tell him I said hello and to give me a social call, not just be an appointment maker." Sharon tilted her head a bit.

"No, no, just a jibe. Great guy, but those hills over there do seem to create a barrier between the Bay and the burbs. Just tunnels connecting them, seems more like walls than passages.

Anyway, Bryan said you had an interesting story about the *Duncan Dynasty*; she came up from Mexico a little busted up. Could have stopped to repair in Long Beach but wanted to keep her schedule and get the repairs done here. Came in and tied up for a few extra days. We pulled the boxes off her stern where the most damage was; PCL had crews all over her within hours and she only missed her departure by one day. Not bad. The totals showed that she lost twenty boxes, a mix of appliances, furniture, some clothing, one guy's Mercedes, some household goods for a diplomat; that gave us more heat than the appliances. Your box was supposed to have farm tools in it, not dead bodies." Sharon must have looked surprised. "I got the word from Cabo two days ago. So you're the woman who caught it; stories like that have legs, become urban legends. Tell me about it."

Sharon repeated the story one more time for Spinos; this time she left out the parts about the kids, the handbags, and her new job. She now worked for STIA; privacy became important.

"Interesting story. It's incredibly rare that a lost container floats for more than a few days. They aren't completely watertight. But they have floated for months if their cargo is buoyant enough or is more air than weight, like tennis shoes or something. They lost the containers just a few days before you found it—big storm, captain says a freak wave did the damage. But why the interest? Why do you care? Nothing about this concerns you."

Good looking or not, he certainly could be irritating. "Professional interest. I've worked a few jobs with Bryan and somehow, go figure, this one has caught my attention. Want to see where it goes. Same thing I told the inspector in Cabo; I'm just interested."

Spinos decided not to push the issue. "Sure, it's your time, not mine; what can I do for you?"

"I wondered where the other two containers on the manifest went after they arrived. Do you have records showing their destinations after they were unloaded?" Sharon asked, in a matter-of-fact way.

"Not sure I should let that information out, somewhat proprietary, but since you and Kevin go back a few years, and I do owe him a favor, I thought you might ask that question." Spinos pulled a sheet of paper out of the top drawer. "They were delivered by the same driver to a warehouse in San Francisco. The address is on 25th Street off Tennessee. I called the driver and he said there was another truck waiting for him when he arrived with the first box; when he returned with the second, the first one was gone. He dropped the container and returned to make a run to Modesto. That's all we have."

"Did you check to see what was inside?"

"Miss O'Mara, we have over two and a half million containers moving through this port every year, almost seven thousand a day. Homeland seems to only be concerned with radiation from boxes, not necessarily what's in them. Customs is overwhelmed, so the simple answer is no. We have a box, a manifest, an address, and a cleared check. After that, it's not our problem. Homeland occasionally makes a big show here and has the National Guard do some training, walk about, drive some Humvees around, carry guns, but they seldom find things. They are all just a pain in the ass and it's all for show."

"Great attitude," Sharon said.

"Hell, we've had dope, drugs, and stolen cars come and go through this port; we don't talk about it, but it's the truth. There isn't enough time and budget to deal with these boxes, to have them searched and properly vetted. I have enough headaches with the Feds and the shipping lines. They want it all now. We also run the airport; only a fool would take on both jobs. Lucky I only have the port." Spinos lifted his two palms in the air and smiled.

"Thanks for your help. Maybe I will take a spin around San Francisco and see what turns up, see what happens."

Spinos walked her back to the lobby and collected her ID badge. He mumbled something else about Bryan, said goodbye and good luck, and walked back through the door that led to the hall that led to his office that led to his desk and the circus that was the port.

5c

Sharon returned to the West Oakland station, went west to San Francisco, and rented a car, hoping the STIA deposit would clear before the bill came; she would drop it off the next day in Walnut Creek. 25th and Tennessee was just south of Mission Bay. New buildings and housing projects were under construction along both sides of 3rd Street on land that, a hundred years earlier, was swamp and tidelands. Now millions of square feet of biomedical office, a new campus for San Francisco State University and thousands of new homes sat on what was once San Francisco Bay. Sharon remembered the Loma Prieta earthquake and shook her head; homes built on Jell-O.

The elevated 580 freeway sat like a thick double-decked ribbon twisting over the one-story mix of pre–World War II warehouses and garages built from galvanized steel, painted wood, and rust. No cars were parked on the potholed streets in the yellow gloom from the streetlights. She could easily count the glowing windows in the buildings. What stood out were the signs—almost all of them were lettered with large Chinese characters with subtitles in English. Shut corrugated steel roll-up garage doors flanked the street, and chain-link gates cut off the alleys. There were no sidewalks.

She drove slowly, looking into the black alleys and the dead ends. After ten minutes, she turned back toward 3rd Street and its traffic and headed downtown. The rental, one of the new hybrids, whined and whirred with its electric motor. "There is no way I will ever get used to this," she thought. She crossed old rail tracks and almost bounced off the roof from the impact of a pothole; the car bottomed out on the asphalt before launching itself in the air. The shocks softened the landing, but it still jarred her. Her STIA-like handbag slid to the floor of the passenger seat.

"Damn it, just fucking great. I rented it, now I busted it," she said out loud. "Damn it."

Sharon pulled to the side of the curb, got out, and walked around the car into the sodium glare of the streetlight. The color of the car was indescribable from the shift in the light spectrum; she saw no damage. An air horn from a truck on the overhead freeway forced her to wince and look past one more chain-link gate sandwiched under the concrete road deck. Through the fence, a streetlight lit the partially obstructed end of a red shipping container; *PCL* reflected off the upper portion of the box's door. Moving to one side, she saw the dark outline of another box jammed in between the first and a concrete block building.

"Well, well, well. What do we have here? Our lost boxes from China?"

She tried to pull open the passenger-side door and it only opened a few inches; it was stuck against the curb. The copy of the manifest that Lopez emailed her and the box numbers of the other containers were on the sheet. She could compare them to the numbers on these to see if they were the same. Returning to the open driver's door, she slid across the center console and tugged her bag free from where it had jammed between the seats. Totally exposed, she suddenly found herself being jerked out of the door and thrown to the street. Her bag snagged on the stick upright on the center console. She instinctively rolled away from the expected kick to her side; it brushed her ribs as it passed.

Rebounding from the asphalt, she spun and kicked hard at the first dark shape that formed; a solid but yielding pressure told her that she had landed a strong blow. A guttural explosion of curses and alcohol washed over her. She backed away, bouncing on her toes, arms out, ready for the next attack; it came from behind. She put her hands up to shield herself from the impact against the open door of the car. She fell hard to her knees, elbows on the seat. *Just give me two seconds,* she thought, as she pushed her hand into the green bag and pulled out the Beretta. Hands grabbed her shoulders and began to spin her around just as her thumb found the safety. The explosion and flash blinded the two men standing in front of her. One turned and immediately ran into the darkness beyond the freeway column; the other, stunned and wobbly, ran his hands over his body to check for blood, and screamed, "You goddamn fucking whore, we was just looking for some fun. Why did you go and have to do that? Fuck." And with that, he turned and, in three steps, disappeared behind the corner of the building.

Sharon's heart raced in time to the thunking of the cars hitting the expansion joints overhead: ka-thunk, ka-thunk, ka-thunk, ka-thunk. The pistol, still gripped in her hand and still aimed at the hole in the pavement two feet from her right shoe, vibrated from an increasing dose of adrenalin she was receiving. Taking a deep breath, she looked about and smiled. "Seen and been through worse in Baghdad. But hell, I certainly didn't need that." She slid the gun back into the bag and pulled out her phone and a small flashlight, quickly dialed her own number, and waited 'til her own recorded message ended. She aimed the flashlight on the end of the first box and read the number into her phone. "Easier than trying to write it down," she said.

New headlights turned on to 25th and the unmistakable flash from the lights on the roof said police to her. She slowly turned to the driver's door and set her purse on the seat, the flashlight slid into her pocket, the phone held tight to her ear.

The prowler slid to a stop. "You okay, ma'am?" the cop on the passenger side asked.

"Just fine, Officer. Hit a damn pothole back there and I pulled over to the side to see if there was any damage. This little baby of mine is new and I was very concerned," she offered, smiling.

"Well, this isn't a good part of town to be doing car inspections. I suggest you move down to 3rd Street, where there are more people and more light. You okay? You look a bit scuffed up."

"I'm fine, stumbled getting out. Thank you for your help and the advice; do you mind following me up 3rd until I get to a better spot, just in case there was any real damage?"

The questioner looked toward his partner, then back at her. "Not a problem. Turn left at the bottom of the hill, then go about a half mile to a small liquor store; that should do, okay?"

"Thank you. That'll be just great, just great."

O'Mara slipped into the driver's seat, slowly closed the door, and, with the imperceptible vibration and whine from the electric engine, headed down the hill to 3rd Street. She pulled into the liquor store's parking lot, waved at the cops, and blew them a kiss. She waited until they turned the corner. Knowing that they probably called her plate in, she quickly headed to the freeway on-ramp, the Bay Bridge, and Walnut Creek. She had no intention of dealing with more police tonight, or having to explain her car situation to them.

5d

Sergeant Nethermann and his two men slowly walked between the gaudy blue and red containers stacked eight high, over sixty-five feet and taller than a five-story building. The aisle between them was exactly sixty feet, just wide enough to drive a fifty-six-foot container down the improvised street of high-rise boxes. All three guardsmen were in urban camouflage, wore helmets, and were armed with M-4s and sidearms. Corporals Dugan and Vaca walked casually, yet with a practiced alertness, flashing their eyes between the rows of boxes; Nethermann held a clipboard. An endless parade of trucks and boxes passed by them at the end of the row; controlled chaos was what Nethermann thought about the scene.

"Should be about here, Vaca," Nethermann said. "The manifest says the box was stacked a week ago, and no one has claimed it." Nethermann walked to the last stack that stood only two high. "That's the one," he said, pointing to the lower container. It was red and the letters *PCL* covered the side.

"This should be the last one today, Sergeant," Vaca said. "Some days this is nothing more than a bizarre scavenger hunt, like a giant lost-and-found. Sergeant, are we ever going to do something exciting?"

"Probably not, Vaca, but after this one I will buy you both a beer before you go home to your kids and the games, second round of March Madness tonight, Cal against Michigan State."

No lock cover on this one, strange, Dugan thought, as he pulled a bolt cutter from his backpack, set the blades against the lock, and cut through the steel like soft butter. Vaca pulled the handles down and swung open the door; the stench hit them hard. Nethermann quickly swung his flashlight into the black space and immediately saw cots, clothes, blankets, and boxes strewn about the floor. The cots held small bodies, women. One hand slowly rose off the edge of the cot and mumbled something. Nethermann didn't hear it; he was yelling into his shoulder mike. "Get the goddamn medics down here, Row 28 north end. I also need ambulances, Oakland PD, Immigration, and the goddamned worthless Custom cops. We have illegals in bad shape . . . No, I don't fucking know where they're from; I only just pulled the fucking door open. Get them all here, now."

Vaca, already in the box, looked closely at the woman on the first cot, thin, emaciated, her skin yellow-white, and ghostlike. He offered his canteen; the girl could barely open her mouth. The few drops he offered settled in her mouth; he watched her swallow. Dugan moved to the others, two on the cots; he made out three others on the floor. The stench of urine and crap filled the air; he put his arm to his face to fight the gagging reflex. He flashed his light into their eyes. Miraculously, they all seemed to be alive; they blinked, but they were just hours from death. The whine of a siren echoed down the steel corridors and magnified until the soldiers couldn't tell its direction.

Dugan watched Nethermann signal to the EMT van as it turned onto their row, waited as it slid to a stop, and pointed into the darkness. Three EMTs jumped from the back and walked quickly into the box; none carried medical boxes. Surprised, they followed as the EMTs began to check on the women. Then Vaca and the Sergeant slowly stood and raised their arms, shaking their heads. He saw Nethermann turn back to face a huge bald man as the butt end of an AK-47 slammed into Sarg's skull. Then he saw the Tasers and that the men holding them were Chinese.

Chapter 6

"**Good afternoon**, Ms. O'Mara. Are you ready for your first day at STIA?" The greeting sounded more like an order than a pleasant welcome. "Put your things in the top drawer, left side of the storeroom, there's a key, that's your drawer," Evelyn Luca said. "No personal items to be left about. Everything to be kept in your drawer and keep it locked."

"As ready as I can be, Ms. Luca," Sharon said, and disappeared into the storeroom behind the glass counters.

Returning, Sharon stood a moment as Luca surveyed her from her red hair pulled in a ponytail to her polished black shoes; between the two, a crisp dark green top with an open neckline with pearl buttons draped loosely over black slacks that coyly hid her athletic body; loop earrings almost touched her shoulders, and a gold belt cinched in at the waist gathered the green silk. The belt caught Luca's and Doris Lau's eyes.

"Excellent, just enough makeup, no clown faces in this shop. Interesting belt," Luca said.

"Bought it in a small gold shop in Dubai; it took a month's pay but, then again, I wasn't sure if I would ever have a chance to wear it, let alone get out of Iraq alive. Arab gold work is unexcelled."

Luca nodded, didn't comment, and turned to Lau. "Doris, please give Sharon a tour of the back room and the basement. Get her a copy of the employee manual and see that she signs in. Then let's see if she remembers how to use a cash register, such as it is."

After a brief tour, the signing of the manual, and a cash machine demonstration, the two stood like overdressed soldiers in front of Luca.

"Did you receive the information you requested, Ms.

O'Mara?" Luca asked.

"Yes, it arrived on Saturday, thank you. The information was very helpful," Sharon said. The information, all fifteen thousand dollars of it, was comfortably sitting in a Union Bank account.

"Ms. Lau, we will see you tomorrow morning at eight; we have a new shipment arriving and the bags need to be inventoried and ID's checked. Thank you for staying late."

"Yes, ma'am, see you tomorrow." Lau looked at Sharon with a cold stare and a nod. "Ms. O'Mara." The door closed slowly and shut with a metallic click.

"Bit of a tight one, that girl," Sharon said.

"She's thorough, efficient, well educated, and she can talk to the warehouse boys in Chinese. That is, when they want to listen. Not sure about those fellows, strutting and preening all the time. They all drive what look like fast and expensive cars; their arms are covered in tattoos. I have her to deal with them. Hard to figure out how they can afford their toys, but that's not my problem."

For the first time in months, Sharon had dressed deliberately that morning. After a coffee breakfast and a walk around the block a few times with Basil, she'd laid out her clothes, showered, put some exotic jell in her hair, clipped on jewelry, and readied herself for a real job. At least she didn't have to start at eight o'clock in the morning; one o'clock suited her just fine on the first day. It was a far cry from the preparation before a patrol in Iraq. Her handbag, the Chinese STIA knockoff, only carried one extra clip; in Baghdad, she carried at least six. She paused for a long moment outside the two-foot-by-six-foot closet and wondered what she would wear tomorrow; she only had enough dressy shop clothes for three days, and then she'd have to wear them for a second time that week. She was quite sure that Luca wouldn't allow the same look more than once a week or maybe even once every two weeks and Sharon absolutely hated black clothing.

"Clothes, I must buy clothes," she said to Basil. "Momma has to look good to catch the bad guys, don't you think?" The green bag hit the dresser with a soft metallic clunk.

Still driving the rental, Sharon parked in the Union Street garage, and scanned the hourly price sheet, now broken into twenty-minute segments. She calculated that the rental car was cheaper to drive by the day than parking it in the garage for the afternoon. She could not afford both options, or, for that matter, either option. God, she wished she still had her green Jaguar. The harsh klaxon of the car behind her woke her from her thoughts and she drove the wedge-shaped car deep into the dark entry of the underground garage.

At precisely two thirty, a tall and extremely well-proportioned blonde walked into the shop on the well-tatted muscular arm of a hard-looking man, ran her hands over the bags on the shelf, and pointed at the largest orange bag. He placed a platinum card in Sharon's palm, waited as she finished with the electronics; they said thank you and left, the bag on one arm, and the other gripped appreciatively on the well-tatted arm. The whole deal took less than ten minutes. Sharon collected a ten percent commission of four hundred and fifty-three dollars, noted the sale in the book under the register, sat down, and wondered about the whole process.

"It can be like that sometimes," Luca said, watching from the stockroom door. "In case you didn't recognize him, he is a very successful rock star that lives in the area. He has bought two bags recently, not surprisingly, for two other women, one a brunette, and the other's hair was more colors than I could identify. Lau will be disappointed that she didn't make the sale."

The rest of the afternoon was quiet, too quiet for Sharon. A couple walked through the shop; the man stood by the door, distracted. She ooh'd and ahh'd, but didn't touch. Tourists. A sharply dressed young man pushed the door open, briefly looked about, spotted Sharon, and noted her glare and her apparent understanding of his trade. He left. Thief was all O'Mara thought about him; being a high-paid store sheriff was boring.

"I'm going to take a look at the warehouse; I need to at some point and this is as good a time as any," Sharon said.

"The gate and the doors are locked; here are the keys. The staff will be gone; it's after five. The two nearest the ring clip open the warehouse; the others are for padlocks hanging in the office." She handed Sharon a card. "Here is my cell number if you need to talk to me; the numbers below it are for the security alarm. Bring the keys back tomorrow; I have my own set."

6b

Sharon was surprised that the warehouse was only one block from where she spotted the containers and was attacked by the bums. In fact, the back of the warehouse abutted the rear of the yard where the red PCL boxes had sat. They were now gone.

In the darkening gloom she saw an old bent chain-link gate guarding a small asphalt lot. A well-rusted steel warehouse sat at the end of the short lot and a roll-up garage door, recently installed by its look, faced the aisle between the barely visible parking stall lines. A steel door stood to the left. Sharon parked just outside the gate on the street. She stuck the Beretta in the small of her back, slid the extra magazine, penlight, and phone into her pockets, and unlocked the gate. Taking a deep breath, she unlocked the door and groped along the interior wall until she found the light switch. She punched in the security code and deactivated the alarm. An office, with high fly-specked windows, stood to the left, and a long row of chain-linked cages followed the office into the darkness, each cage filled with cardboard boxes; manifest papers were stapled to small panels on each door. To the right and in the middle of the parking bay, serviced by the roll-up doors, stood two red shipping containers; the white letters *PCL* stood out in the glare of the overhead halogen lights.

"Well, well, well, what do we have here?" Sharon retrieved her phone from her handbag and looked through her photo archive. She tapped on the photo she wanted, noted the info on the box in the photo, and the info on the box sitting in the bay—both were identical. "Now why would these be here? I doubt they're hiding from their missing brother lying at the bottom of the ocean somewhere off the coast of Cabo. Whatever they are, they obviously didn't contain the same message left in the Mexican box," she said out loud.

The front door rattled; she ducked behind the first container and watched as two men pushed the door open.

"I told you. I turned the fucking lights off!" the taller one said.

"Well, they didn't turn themselves back on," the fat man answered. "The security alarm is off; you forget that, too?"

"No, I turned it on and set everything."

Sharon slowly walked out from between the boxes.

Fat Boy saw her first. "Who the fuck are you, and how'd you get in here?"

The two seemed to stiffen a bit and visibly brace themselves after seeing O'Mara; they also blocked the only way out.

"That's my question to you boys; who are you? No one is supposed to be here after five and yet there you stand. Now, who are you?" Always better to start out a conversation on the aggressive side.

"No fucking way, you first." Sharon noticed for the first time that both of the boys were Chinese.

"In an effort to move this along, boys, I'm Evelyn Luca's new salesperson and she asked me to come out here and become familiar with the inventory and the access process. There, I've showed you mine—now it's your turn."

The two looked at each other, then at Sharon. The taller one said, "We work here; we went out for a beer after work and noticed the lights were on when we passed by. Decided to see what was up, thought it might have been Luca."

"Well, as you can see, it's not. I'll close up, you can go," Sharon said in her most dismissive manner. "There's no reason to stick around. I'll tell Ms. Luca all about your dedication to your job." She could tell they were nervous, no need to push it. "Go on, I'll be fine. You can go."

The two slowly turned to the door; the light from the overhead window finally shined on their faces. Tall Boy's mug was almost split in two by a scar from just above the left eye to the chin. The pudgier man's tee shirt barely hid the outline of the pistol stuck in the back of his baggy trousers. Sharon heard the lock set in the door after they left.

Sharon waited ten slow beats, her eyes never leaving the door.

"I wonder, Bob," she said out loud to the empty cages. "I think I'll choose box number one—the grand prize just has to be there. Yes, well let's just see what I've won, Bob." A large padlock secured the doors. Sharon quickly sorted through the keys until she found a likely candidate, tried the lock, and, to her shock, it clicked open. "Well, this is a surprise."

The box was empty, too empty. She flashed the penlight around the interior and walked to the back casting the light to the ceiling and the walls. Nothing. Heading to the next box, she stopped short before she reached the end of the container, shook her head, and walked back to the open doorway. She looked down the side of the container and then back inside. Taking toe-to-heel steps, she paced out the floor of the box's interior. She then did the same to the outside; the outside measurement was eight steps longer. She returned to the interior, walked to its end, and looked closely along the edges. A small wire hung loosely from one edge of the folded steel panel; a piece of loose black tape had once hid the wire. She tugged and the wire drew easily toward her. Instantly, the whole panel wall began to open slowly. Stepping back, she allowed the panel to fall along its hydraulically controlled descent. The familiar armory smell of gun oil filled her nose. She recognized immediately what was contained in the twenty-odd heavy boxes filling the smuggler's hole.

The warehouse door slammed and Sharon spun toward the sound. Two silhouettes were outlined by the overhead lights.

"Lady, you're too damn fucking nosey for your own good; that's what I told Chin here—that broad is too damn fuck'en nosey, right! I said that, right?" Fat Boy said.

"Yeah, you did; sure as fuck did," his partner agreed.

"Well, what are we gonna do with you? Can't leave you

here; can't take you with us." The pistol was no longer stuck in the boy's pants; he gripped it firmly, and it hung loosely to one side.

"You can just forget that you saw me and we can let this all pass, as if this never happened. I can keep my mouth shut, I know how," Sharon said, pushing a fearful shutter into her voice. The boys' arrival shook her; she usually never missed the clues. These guys were good.

"I have never known a bitch to keep her lips shut, let alone a nosey one who knows shit. They just seem to have to tell someone, right, Chin?" The tall scarred boy nodded.

She wanted them to come to her; she didn't want to go to them. They were cocky and, even though they were on guard, to them she was just a stock girl, a nobody.

"Out," Chin said. "Now, slowly."

"No, I'm staying right here."

"Like hell you are. Pull her out," Fat Boy said.

Scarface headed toward her, his long shadow moving along the iron floor. Fat Boy covered his advance. she waited, intentionally throwing her eyes around the room, hands fluttering about. As expected, Scarface walked directly into Fat Boy's line of fire. At that instant, she stepped hard and fast into Scarface, slammed her knee into his crotch, threw her open palm into his throat, and, with an upward stab, tried to crush his Adam's apple. A loud explosion filled the box. Scarface screamed through his crushed larynx, and Sharon felt blood and tissue from his exploded shoulder spray her face. She pulled the Beretta from its elastic nest and, with her shoulder down like a 49er lineman, pushed Scarface as fast as she could toward Fat Boy. Sharon shoved the pistol under Scarface's worthless arm and fired at Fat Boy; the bullet impacted the roll-up door. Fat Boy spun out of the container and fired wildly into blackness; the round ricocheted throughout the box until it embedded itself in one of the cartons. Sharon heard the door slam as she dumped Scarface on the deck. She took a deep breath, wiped the blood splatter off her face, and pulled the cell phone from her pocket.

The police arrived three minutes after her call, and the EMTs followed two minutes later. Scarface would survive, just barely. He would be very hoarse for a long time, but he came within a half inch of being dead; the bullet missed his carotid artery by that much. His shoulder would need reconstruction; the pistol Fat Boy fired was at least a .44 caliber, not a toy. ATF was called, as well as Homeland and the FBI. In two hours it looked like a convention of national police agencies: blue and white uniforms, plainclothes, and San Francisco police. Sharon sat in a cheap plastic chair and watched the circus. Shiny nylon jackets with reflective white or yellow letters painted on the back walked about in the dark corners of the warehouse.

"You were the woman I saw last week, not a block from here. Something about a pothole or something?" the beat cop said to O'Mara, as the feeding frenzy continued.

"Yeah, it was me," she said.

"Your car came up as a rental. Would have done something then but you were gone and I didn't have the time to chase you down. Now what's the real skinny here?"

"Between you and me, I was down here looking at the inventory. I work for the company that rents the space and these two walked in on me."

"And you just happen to carry a Beretta?"

"A girl needs protection these days, Officer; you just never know."

6c

"Why the hell didn't they kill us, Lieutenant? We should all be dead; hell, if we were in Iraq, we would all be dead, throats cut or worse. Why the hell only knock us out?"

"Don't know, Nethermann, sometimes you're lucky. Vaca and Dugan say that after they knocked you down, the first two EMTs fired Tasers at them and put them on the deck. From there they watched three of them, all Chinese, carry the women from the box to the van; the fourth stood cover. They were gone in less than three minutes. Vaca was the first to get to his feet. A second ambulance pulled up and Vaca says he put his rifle to his shoulder and waited. The EMTs, the real ones, were shocked to see someone pointing a gun at them. They put their arms up, and security and the cops quickly filled the aisle between the boxes. That's about when you woke up."

"Goddamn, Lieutenant, what the hell is this all about?"

"Slavery, Sergeant. Those girls were sent here to be sex slaves. This isn't the first time we've found these boxes; but this is the closest we have come to catching them."

"Should be easy to track the box. All the paperwork and sensors and shit are here."

"Yes, and we know where it started, from a port near Hong Kong. But how it got there, who paid who to make sure no one remembers, and the fine help from the Chinese government have hidden it all from American questions."

"How many?" Nethermann asked.

"From the evidence in the box, we counted seven. They had water and food for the trip; they didn't count on it being lost for almost two weeks after arriving. Why they didn't try to signal or make noise, I don't know. One of the investigators says the girls are told that, if they're caught by the Americans, they will be put in prison or worse. They're usually told they're going to get good jobs and make a lot of money. So my guess is they waited, but by then it was too late."

"The Chinese?"

"Seems they must have known that there was a search being made for their box. They waited outside the gate, out of sight. We think there's inside information being passed on to these gangs. They heard your call over the radio and pulled through the front gate before the real EMTs—they cut it real close. A few minutes later and they wouldn't have made it through. These guys are well connected and they are pros. The Feds are sure they're part of a large network of smugglers and counterfeiters, Chinese run, with possible connections to Eastern Europe and Italy. It's just one big happy fucking family."

"They didn't kill us because that would have brought in one

more layer of bullshit, I guess," Nethermann said. "Just lucky this time, real lucky."

"Yeah, real lucky. Vaca also says that the one who slugged you, the big bald one, was a mean-looking son of a bitch; another was fat but moved fast; the others were hard, a real tough-looking bunch, didn't say a word to each other the whole time. He said they all flashed a square tattoo on their right forearm, near their elbow. Couldn't make it out, but it was red."

Chapter 7

O'Mara's cottage was a short walk to BART and the center of Walnut Creek. The style was California bungalow; gray green stucco walls held up the reshingled roof, and the front door was a dark red, almost burgundy. The door led to a short hall that collected the various rooms along its length until it tumbled past the kitchen and into the rear yard, Basil's domain. The small living room held bookshelves, comfortable furniture, and a fireplace. The two bedrooms, really only one, the other was her office, were snug and colorfully painted in a soft green that carried the colors from the garden to the inside. The kitchen allowed her the space she needed to cook and entertain in an elegant, albeit limited, manner. She knew every corner and doorway, even in the dark. She was happy here.

But Ms. Evelyn Luca was not happy. The beat cop was not happy. Scarface was not happy and was not talking. The only people acting happy were ATF and Homeland Security—for them it was Christmas. The twenty heavy-duty cardboard boxes contained one hundred and sixty Chinese-made, fully automatic Type 81 assault rifles, almost a match to the AK-47, but made in China to military specs and quality; they were in excellent shape, brand new and scary as all hell. What these guns could do in the hands of drug dealers and the scum wandering about in the back alleys of the United States was something Sharon didn't want to think about; in Mexico they could lead to revolution. Kevin got this information through his contacts at Oakland police. All very hush-hush; the Feds didn't want the story out on the street. They wanted more and were hoping, by holding back a lot of the facts, that they would find it. She wasn't so sure.

"Luca was livid, Kevin. Thought she was going to explode,"

Sharon said. "The Feds sealed her warehouse, the store is shut for the next week, and her family in Italy is probably not happy either. She's even under suspicion; you know how it is, shut everything down. Then sort it out, no matter what the damage."

"It was all going on right under her nose; a bit naïve, don't you think?"

"Good businesswoman; left the warehouse to others. Doris Lau, who worked there, disappeared that afternoon. Her address was as fake as her story. She was the inside guy, as they say. Yes, Luca was naïve and was caught by it."

Basil rubbed up against Sharon's arm; she set the glass of cabernet on the coffee table and took a dry toast from the plate of tomato bruschetta and offered it to him. "Good boy, go lay down." Basil, the toast held gently in his lips, curled up on his bed at the end of the couch. His eyes never left her, even when he set his huge head on the edge of the foam cushion. Only then did he crack the toast in two.

"There is a surge of this stuff, according to Oakland and the port; they found two other containers full of fake goods. Handbags, scarves, some jewelry, and even boxes full of toys. A couple of the real manufacturers sent their people out to take a look and were impressed until they looked inside; they said the guts were junk and would last until midday Christmas, at best. But then again, what toy survives past Christmas, anyway? They called it smugglers day—Christmas. Everything is pushed through to get it sold for Christmas, here and in Europe."

"Just great, preying on poor unsuspecting grandparents buying more junk for their grandkids—just another reason why I'm not a big fan of the current version of Christmas."

"Yeah, I know. But the toy guys say it takes millions of dollars out of their pockets."

"I rest my case," Sharon said, with a smirk. "I wonder how this connects to the four dead men in Cabo? The box was the third in the set; the other two ended up at STIA's warehouse, but empty. The second container also had a hidden compartment, but had already been cleared out. Residuals also suggest there may have been weapons, but ATF still isn't sure. Why the dead guys?"

"A message is my guess, but not a difficult one, and, remember, these guys here didn't get that message. So someone is still pissed at someone here and my guess is they still need to send that message.

"The Feds found a box full of fake RFID markers in Lau's locked drawer at the shop," Kevin continued. "She was probably going to insert them in the fake bags and then pass them off as the real thing. Where they were going, no one knows, yet. The thinking is that she was sending the real bags somewhere, selling them as legit handbags because they were, and pocketing the money—STIA never knew. The fakes were passed off here as the real thing. Why she thought Luca wouldn't find out, we're not sure. The Feds say that Lau is in the wind, at least for now."

"Guns and handbags, all the things you need to start a war."

Over the next hour, Sharon prepared a small feast of spinach salad and chicken risotto. Another cabernet was opened and Kevin talked about one of his survivors. The young girl, alone after the murder of her father, was starting St. Mary's in the fall. She wanted to be a journalist. How she got that idea, he wasn't sure, but the child had grown into a beautiful young lady. Her future looked far brighter than the one she faced ten years earlier.

"She met a couple of great people in the chaos after the shooting," Kevin said. "One was a reporter from one of the TV stations and, between the two of us, we helped her find a place to stay and eased her back into school and eventually she finished high school. Touch and go for a while, but she's tough, and proud of what she did."

"I'm sure you had a lot to do with how she turned out," Sharon added. "To you." She lifted her glass. Kevin's cheeks blushed from both pride and wine. His eyes looked heavy.

"You, sir, are sleeping on the couch. Then you can leave early when you're better off. I have a busy day tomorrow and I can't babysit."

Kevin drained the last of the wine, helped clear the table, found the familiar sheets and pillows, and quickly fell asleep. Basil sniffed his cheek and looked at Sharon.

"He'll be fine, go to bed now." Basil took his usual spot just outside her bedroom door, where he had a view through the length of the house. Sharon turned the light out.

7b

In the blackness Sharon could only make out the darker head of Basil pushing against her cheek. His impatient nudge had awakened her; she laid still and listened. The familiar mechanical screeching from the BART train disappeared into the night. Basil's breathing and a muffled scrunching, through the cracked window, was all she heard.

"Good boy, quiet now, quiet." Basil turned toward the door. Sharon extracted the Beretta from the holster on the bed stand. A tall shadow stood in the door.

"You awake?" Kevin said in a whisper.

"Yes. Did you hear it, too?"

"Yes, and a shadow passed by the front window. You expecting someone?"

"Too early for trick-or-treaters." Sharon saw the unmistakable glint of his pistol.

The house seemed to breathe in and out for a four count, and then held its breath. The three stood, like they were waiting for the gates of hell to open; then from both ends of the hallway the explosions of splintering doors and gunfire shattered the night. Four men charged into the house, two through each doorway, firing down the length of the hall. O'Mara and Bryan stood off to one side as bullets flew through the house. In the light show of gunfire, the front-door assassins managed to hit one of their own men; he went down quietly. The remaining three slowly worked their way through the rooms, scanning each with their flashlights, until all that was left was Sharon's bedroom.

"The bitch has got to be in there." His answer was one hundred pounds of pissed-off dog in his face. Sharon had tried to hold Basil back, keeping him still. But that only lasted so long; he broke free of her to defend his mistress.

The man's scream broke the momentary silence; Basil had caught him high on his shoulder and had a part of his cheek, neck, and ear in his mouth. Kevin fired past Basil and into the two that remained standing. She fired lower and at their legs, or at least what she thought were legs. More bullets flew past her head; she heard the mirror over her dresser explode.

Unprepared for the massive defense, the two men backed out the front door, firing down the hall; the third lay on the floor, Basil's body draped over him. The fourth didn't move. Kevin turned on the hall light. Sirens could be heard and they were getting louder.

"Shit, goddamit, shit," Kevin said. "The bastards just couldn't wait until the cavalry arrived; called them on my cell when I first saw the shadows." He turned toward Sharon but she was gone. He looked at the mess in the hall. She was on the floor cradling Basil.

"He's hurt badly, Kevin. We need to get him to the hospital, now."

"John Muir, and I don't give a damn what they say. As far as I'm concerned, he's a police dog tonight."

Three cops came through the door, guns drawn. Bryan's "officer on scene" prepared them for the badge he held high. They understood when he picked up the dog and carried him out the door; the ride in the back of the prowler was loud and crowded as they raced up Ygnacio Boulevard to the hospital. Basil's pained whimpers broke Sharon's heart as she held her best friend's head.

7c

Sharon never left Basil's side during the night. Kevin returned to the house with the cop who had driven them to the hospital.

"I'll take care of the questions and answers or at least until you can get there," he said before he left Sharon. "The neighborhood will be up in arms about now. I'll see what I can do to find out who the hell they were."

"I bet I know, but I'll wait until I hear from you." Sharon held up her cell phone.

The street was a police parking lot. Kevin counted eight squad cars and the step-van that the town used for the SWAT team. Lights were set up on the lawn; the house was floodlit. Maybe a hundred neighbors stood just outside the yellow tape that was quickly run between the trees and secured. Flashes from cameras stabbed the night and mixed with the blue and white staccato of lights from the police cars. The coroner's SUV was parked directly in front of the door. Lights were on in all the front rooms. He held up his badge and walked through the four officers standing on the entry walk.

"You okay, Kevin? And Sharon?" a tall officer asked, as he worked his way down the hall.

"Hi, Marty. Yeah, just peachy. Not a scratch. Sharon is at John Muir."

"She hurt?"

"No, but her dog was shot in the back hip by one of these assholes. The doc saw the honorary K-9 Squad collar he wore and there was not even a question. Lost blood, but nothing shattered, real lucky. If he were killed, I'm not sure what she would've done. What's happening here, Marty?"

Sergeant Kline pointed to the first body in the hall. "That one is some of the dog's handiwork. Shit, never seen a man with his throat ripped out. That dog was something possessed, but that fellow also had the most firepower; a Type 81 was under his body, Chinese, never seen one before. One of the men knew the rifle, looks new."

"Only heard pistols. If they had opened up with that, not sure any of us would be alive. The other?" Kevin pointed toward the far end of the corridor.

"Bled out, shot in the chest. Did you get him?"

"Not sure. There were maybe fifty or sixty rounds fired." He looked at the pockmarks on the walls, and quickly counted eighteen. "I fired a full clip, not sure how many Sharon fired." He saw a Beretta on the floor; a numbered cone stood next to it. "That's probably hers."

Kline made a note on a small pad. They walked the length of the hall to the outside, carefully walking around the shell casings that littered the hardwood. Two more techs passed them on their way into the house.

"We found a blood trail from here—" Kline pointed at the doorsill—"that led to the sidewalk and then up the street. It stopped near that 'No Parking' sign, probably where they parked, nothing after that. We have alerts to all the hospitals, was a good amount of blood. If he doesn't get help, then there's a chance we may never find him alive. What went on here, Kevin? Not your usual way to end an evening."

Kevin told him everything about the evening. He also told him briefly about Sharon finding the guns in the warehouse.

"You think they're related?"

"Absolutely. That rifle under the kid may prove it. They found over a hundred similar 81s in the container. My guess is that someone is very pissed that they were lost and wanted to extract a bit of revenge. Too bad they didn't realize that they were just a few hours late for dinner," Kevin said with a smile. "Good dinner, too, chicken risotto. Sharon can cook like a Food Channel pro."

"You two finally dating?"

"Mind your own business, Marty, and I won't hurt you. As always, we are just friends, just friends."

"Then why were you here at two in the morning? I got to ask, Kevin."

"For dinner and I was just a little under the influence; I know how tough you guys are, so I was sleeping on the couch. Got up to take a pee and saw a shadow cross the window; lucky for me that I drank too much. Who knows what would have happened. Sharon and the dog were ready—lucky, just damn lucky. Those two back there weren't—thought they'd catch us by surprise."

Kevin called Sharon and told her everything he had learned.

She asked about the house.

"Looks like a good Swiss cheese with marinara sauce on the floor."

"Great, never was much into housecleaning; now it's house repair and cleaning," Sharon said.

"I know a good crime scene guy and contractor; I'll call him in the morning. Basil?"

"Resting. They gave him a sedative. Doctor says he will have a good limp for a while but in time he should heal and be none the worse for it all. They did all they could do for him, but I have to bring him home in the morning. They gave me a little latitude because of the police connection, but they could only go so far. The hospital staff didn't make a ruckus; just glad they were there. Even had some canine blood as a backup to the Walnut Creek K-9s. I'll stay here till midmorning. Can you come and get me? I'll take Basil home then."

"See you at ten."

Kevin walked back through the scene. The techs had one dead man on a gurney, a lanky Chinese man. He looked at the face. The left side was shredded, ear laid back; he saw bone. The man's eyes held a look of fear and surprise. One arm was exposed to the elbow, a square red tattoo embedded on the inside forearm. The other body, at the end of the hall, was being zippered into a long black bag. Kevin studied the man's face, also Chinese.

"Would you open the bag to the man's right arm?" Kevin asked the CSI.

The tech pulled up the arm with his latex-gloved hand; rigor mortis had begun to set in. He rolled the arm and the same tattoo slowly appeared; a one-inch red square box held an obvious Chinese character. Kevin could not make it out; he understood a few symbols from his Oakland PD days, but not this one.

"Blood," the CSI offered.

"Yeah, everywhere, I know," Kevin answered.

"No, sir, that's the Chinese character for blood."

Only then did Kevin notice that the tech was Oriental.

"You sure?"

"Absolutely, Officer. My great-grandmother came here to be with her husband when the railroads were built—she was one of the few. They survived; she made sure her children and grandchildren never forgot their homeland. All of us speak, write, and read Chinese. This character is pronounced 'xue.' It means blood. I noticed it on the other body as well. Gangs tat their soldiers to ensure fealty and family. This is a new one to me. But my guess is that it's only new to us. These guys, from the look of the teeth and complexion, didn't grow up around here. They are Chinese by birth and they spent a good chunk of their lives in the homeland. Why they ended up here is for you to find out."

"Your name?"

"Stanley Chen of the Chen dynasty, just love to say that," Stanley said with a smile. "Don't know you but I saw you a few months ago at that BART killing; Bryan, isn't it?"

"Kevin Bryan, Lafayette police." They didn't shake hands.

"Good to finally meet you. Neat bit of work there; also cleaned up that condo building thing. They say the name here is O'Mara, Sharon O'Mara?" Kevin nodded. "Going to stay near you, Officer Bryan—your activity will always ensure that I have a job." He smiled at Kevin but Kevin didn't smile back.

"You seem to be a bit out of your jurisdiction, if I may ask?"

"You may, but only professionally. I was having dinner here with a friend. Then all hell broke loose. Anything else on these guys?"

"No wallets or IDs. Clothing nondescript, nothing to identify them with. That one was a load to get on the gurney, must weigh close to three hundred pounds; took four of us to get him on the damn thing. America has been good to him, all fattened up. This fellow—" Chen pointed to the bag on the floor—"I would guess has been here only a short time, still thin, shows a touch of jaundice and malnutrition; we will confirm that at the autopsy. His tattoo is also new; the hair around it had not grown back over the stain, less than three months old."

"Thanks, Stanley. Can you make sure that I get a copy of the report?"

"I'll clear it with Walnut Creek, but usually it's no problem. I know Sharon from the range. How's the dog?"

"You're a box of surprises, Stanley Chen. They're both okay. She's wasn't hit, but her dog, Basil, caught a slug in the rear end. She says he'll be fine. But I can tell you whoever set this up is going to be in a world of hurt. You don't shoot her dog and get away with it."

Chapter 8

The noise from the contractors was finally over for the day. Sharon sat at her computer and caught up on the latest news and emails. Basil, with a bandage still wrapping his butt, slept on his bed, one eye open.

Kevin had passed on the coroner's reports and everything the police found. The fat kid turned out to be the same fellow Sharon had run into at the warehouse. Not only had Basil wreaked damage on the man, but a bullet from Bryan's service pistol had torn a hole through his chest. The coroner believed he was dead before the dog's damage would have killed him. He was a Chinese national, lived in Oakland, had loose gang affiliations and a few juvenile reports; obviously he had moved up the food chain.

The other was definitely Chinese but had no identification—nothing. He was not on any database or immigration lists. Nothing. It's as if the man existed, but not in any real-world sense; Sharon believed this was intentional. A soldier with no history is hard to track; there is no trail to follow. Still, after three weeks, the bodies had not been claimed. Scarface refused to even acknowledge that he knew the fat boy who had the name William Yong on his passport; he was from Dongguan, about fifty miles from Hong Kong. His entry papers had him listed as a student, eight years earlier, and since then, nothing. Luca's paperwork on him and his social security number were as fake as the documents from Miss Lau.

"Tight little family here," Sharon said to Basil. "I think I know what they're into, but I wonder what else I'm missing." A quick online tour of Bing and Google gave her more information about Dongguan and the region than she could handle. The region contained three or four times the population of California

and there were tens of thousands of small businesses and manufacturers located there. "My guess is that there are a couple
of handbag makers and armament factories among them, a nice
mix."

The week after the shooting was chaotic with construction
crews working and cleanup taking place all at the same time.
The cleaning of the sauce on the floor was the easiest. The holes
in the walls were another matter. She thought the holes in the
walls could be easily patched, until the contractor opened up
one area; lath and plaster is more difficult to fix than modern
drywall. Bullets had ripped into the electrical wiring. The double wires of the original construction were not to code and the
contractor had to replace wiring as he opened the walls, then
close them up. Some bullets traveled through three walls before
stopping. They found two slugs in the panel over the fireplace.
They came from the rear-door thugs.

Two weeks and $25,000 in insurance and deductibles later,
she had a new interior, one that wasn't planned for. It did give
her a chance to change the color scheme. She would have preferred to just buy a hundred dollars' worth of paint.

Her cell phone began to tone the Mexican cockroach song;
Sharon stared at the screen and wrinkled her forehead. "Basil,
this will be a very weird, strange call."

"Sharon O'Mara," she answered, knowing full well who
was on the other end."

"Buenos Dias, Señorita. How is my favorite American gringo detective?"

"Good morning, Inspector Detective Xavier Lopez, how are
you?" She looked at Basil and rolled her eyes; he cocked his head
and shrugged, as if a dog could shrug.

"Excellent, magnifico, and you?"

"Good." She didn't want to spend the next hour recapping
the last two weeks, even if it was his dime.

"Are you available for lunch next Saturday? I will be in town
for a meeting and would be honored to have another delicioso
meal with you. I'm here to help your local police answer a few

questions about our container and its connection to the weapons found in San Francisco."

"Xavier, that was not our box or anyone's; it found us." She flashed on him marching down the stone steps of the hotel, all puffed up like a generalissimo. Since that first impression, she had mellowed a bit. He was a lot of pomp and circumstance but also a reasonably good cop in a shitty neighborhood.

"True, true, but it really makes no difference. She is ours now and your government wants to know what I know. They said that you were helpful, but now they need expert help, so voila." She could hear the humor in his voice. "And besides, I can finally eat in a good restaurant and not be worried about being shot by the help, si?"

"Si, I mean yes. No, wait a minute, hold on." She took a deep breath. "Now, as for lunch, that sounds great. Saturday at the Waterfront on Broadway—noon, okay? I assume this is an expense report lunch?"

"Si, your government is very grateful for my assistance." Again his tone suggested Mexican irony.

"Then I will see you there, and we can catch up. It has been a very busy month so far."

"*Que?*"

"Later, Detective, adios."

"Till then, adios, Sharon O'Mara."

Basil looked at his mistress. "Well, that was a shot out of the blue. Who would have thought he would tango his way back into my life? Not sure whether it's a good thing or just a strange thing." Basil laid his head back on his bed; he wondered the same thing.

8b

Doris Lau, alias Pinkie, stood over the man that was held down by three large powerful men. The man looked up at the woman, with her streak of pink hair hanging over one eye, as he pleaded for mercy. Feng stood next to her, smiling.

"It was Yong's fault," the man whined in Chinese. "It was

his idea to rush from both sides; we didn't know a devil dog and two people with guns were there. It was stupid—he deserved to die."

"You little sniveling toad, he was my cousin, watch your mouth."

Feng knew he was right; Yong had screwed up once too much. The warehouse was a big screw-up and this attack cost him his life. It would add to the heat on the business. He knew that Lau didn't need this.

"Knife," she ordered, holding out her hand like a surgeon.

"No, it will not happen again. No. No, it will not happen—I promise."

"I believe you, Yunxu, but you will need a reminder, a reminder that you will always carry with you."

Lau took the blade from one of the men and brought it down sharply across his little finger. The severed finger threw blood across both tattoos, one on the man's damaged arm and the other on Doris Lau's forearm.

The men wrapped the hand, and hustled the whimpering man out of the room.

"Now what?" Feng said. "This is getting out of hand and all too quickly. I told you to watch Yong. Told you he was a hothead and getting worse." The man crossed his sinewy arms over his massive chest, his tattoo was obvious.

"Yes, Feng," Lau said. "I don't need your assessment to make me more aware of it. They were impatient and fucked it up. Unfortunately, now the police and the Feds know a little more about us, more than they should. We can do nothing about that, but we can stop them from learning anything more. I want our contacts to learn nothing, nothing. And if they ask, don't tell them anything; it is hard to follow a trail when there are no crumbs."

Feng rolled his eyes toward the metal ceiling as he left the room. The pay was good and his status in the family was secure—hell, she was his American cousin. But a college degree and a teenage life spent in San Fernando didn't necessarily make her the best to lead the clan's West Coast operations. Sometimes you need to use force to make a point; that was what Yong was trying to do, but he was stupid. *Now we have lost three men. We can recruit more but never the kind that family blood can insure, like the blood on his arm. Loyalty, honor, and obedience are all I ask from my men. These I can only get from China, where fear is the best insurance. Sure, she's smart, but book smart. Sometimes muscle is needed as well.* Feng pushed his way past the two men supporting the maimed man.

"Get the physician to stitch him up. I need you two in an hour. Meet me at the warehouse. Leave him at the old house; I'll talk to him later."

The two shook their collective heads. Feng climbed into his black Mercedes and left the warehouse. The noise from the Nimitz Freeway covered the sound of his tires squealing, as he spun onto Derby Ave.

8c

Sharon looked at the face of her phone as it started playing "*O Sole Mio.*" "This ought to be fun. Sharon O'Mara," she said, after pushing on the side of the Bluetooth stuck in her ear. The tune was set to her former boss's number.

"Miss O'Mara, Evelyn Luca. We need to talk. I realize all this crap was not your fault, sorry for the outburst. But I was very pissed; in fact, I still am, and they still aren't sure when I will get my shop back."

"I understand, but what happened could have been worse. I think you were lucky."

"You're the lucky one; you could have been killed. We need to talk. There're many things I need to know, things that were kept hidden, and maybe you can help."

"I still have a job? After the Feds and all, not sure if you wanted to see my face again."

"I'm sure that we're not the only ones listening to this call. There may be some things you can help me with."

"Let's assume we're not alone. Are you free for lunch today?

Perry's on the Embarcadero; you know it?"

"Yes, say twelve thirty?"

"See you then."

Sharon finished washing the dishes. "Well, mister, it looks like the old lady's luncheon dance card is starting to fill up. Two free lunches this week. I think I need to start working on my dinner card." Basil put his head back on his bed and closed his eyes.

The past few weeks had been rough on her wardrobe, and she left the cottage in jeans and a high-collared heavy black silk top, informally dressy. Good enough for lunch in town; the orange faux STIA bag finished the look. She thought about San Francisco fifty years earlier when no self-respecting lady would show up in town without a hat and gloves. Now dressing up, for some, meant showing a little less tattooed arm and pimping up your hair to vertical.

She also grabbed a couple of cloth bags before she walked to BART. Tuesday was the weekday farmers market at the Ferry Building, a chance to replenish her herbs and vegetables. Tomatoes were just coming into season and so were peaches. She told Basil there was marinara and cobbler in his future.

Midday BART is a dream compared to the morning and evening chaos. She had a choice of seats and the arrival time matched the schedule. Ferry Plaza was bathed in sunshine with a light breeze off the water. She stopped for a small Peets coffee and collected the latest Robert Dugoni book at Book Passage. The market was still thinly populated, but lunchtime was still an hour away. Tourists mingled and loitered among the stands and tables, taking photos with early melons and zucchini. Sharon watched the ancient trolley cars as they rattled past, heading toward Fisherman's Wharf. The Giants were on the road in Chicago, so the crowds usually heading to the midweek games would not return until they came home. "San Diego," she said, reminding herself of their next homestand, as she stuffed a bundle of basil and celery into her bag. Two slices of pork tenderloin from the rotisserie truck and she would arrive at the restaurant right on time.

She walked over to the railing and lit a cigarette, even though she was sure she was in violation of some do-gooder law passed in this town. A white and blue ferry churned water as it backed away from the pier; Larkspur was its destination. A few stragglers, mostly tourists, walked out of the Ferry Building and headed up the Embarcadero toward Fisherman's Wharf.

The walk to Perry's took all of five minutes and she took a seat in the outside area, the table still bathed in late morning sunshine. Feeling well, she ordered a Bloody Mary and chomped on a breadstick. Luca, as always, was prompt.

"Well, Ms. O'Mara, you're something," she said, ordering a glass of pinot noir. "First, Mexico, then, my warehouse, and then, I hear, your house. This isn't an accident, is it, or is there always a dark cloud following you?"

Sharon smiled and asked, "Calamari?"

"Absolutely." Luca waved to the waiter and placed their order, just as the drinks arrived. "To you, one hell of a broad. I didn't know what I was getting when you walked into my shop with that bag. Probably should have told you to turn your butt around and leave, but there you were and here we are. Salute."

Sharon smiled at the strange left- and right-hand compliments and comments. "Yes, it has been an interesting few weeks. Now, what do you want me to do for you? Probably couldn't screw it up any worse than I have already."

"Well, you still have a few dollars left on the retainer and I need you to read this before we go any further. It might change your mind." Evelyn Luca slipped an envelope from her burgundy handbag; the STIA badge flashed in the sun that was starting to retreat over the rooftop.

Sharon opened the envelope and extracted a handwritten note in English; the penmanship was excellent. It was a PDF copy of the original.

"The original?" she asked.

"It was sent to my email address; the cover letter said to erase the file and make sure the history is erased. I did that."

"Hard to intercept an email; hard to follow. They knew your

phone and mail were being watched." She went back to the PDF.

Ms. Luca,

You were very fortunate to have escaped all of these tribulations without losing your life. There are some who wished to use a heavier hand but I talked them out of it for old time's sake. But beware; even though you may think you're through with me, there are others I have less control over. If you wish to remain alive, I still need your assistance in a few matters of interest dealing with some cargoes I need to receive. Your help in this matter would be appreciated. I will get in touch.

Doris Lau

"Without a doubt, this is one of the ballsiest notes I've ever read, or one of the stupidest. Where did this land?"

"My house. She has my email address. I pulled it off the server after I printed it. I have a copy on an encrypted memory stick. Any information I can delete has been deleted."

"My guess is that she sent it to let you know a few things. One, she doesn't want to let go of you. Two, she still has things in the pipeline that she needs to unload somehow, and three, your import license still carries weight. Oh, and lastly, she emailed it because she's sure that your phones are tapped."

"You think so? I thought all the legal things were behind me."

"I doubt that. Once the Feds have an information source, they will not give it up until it's dry. That's why it was emailed—a lot harder to track and follow it back to its source."

"That's possible, but it scares the crap out of me and pisses me off. That's why I called you. I need to get my shop open and I need to get my warehouse back. Every day costs me and STIA thousands in lost revenue. That may not mean much to you but it does to me and my partners."

"Whoa, girl, I understand. And money always means something to me. Yes, there may be some things I can do but I also suggest that you wait a while. The Feds are not here to help; they have a different agenda. Getting your shop and warehouse back may help you, but their goal is to find the whole operation. That letter from Pinkie . . ."

"Pinkie? You mean Doris Lau?"

"Yes, I called her that from the first day, sorry."

"No, it fits, puts a different and more interesting perspective to her."

"That letter confirms it to Homeland and Customs. They will watch and wait, but not long. I suggest you disappear for a while, make it hard for Lau to find you; she can't leverage you if she can't control you. I don't give the Feds that much credit either—they are a bureaucracy and it takes time to roll things through their systems."

"I don't run from anything."

"I didn't say run. I said to just disappear for a while, maybe until this is over. You need to stay out of their way."

"I can go to Italy."

"I doubt the Feds will let you out of the country; they need you here to tease out the thugs. You probably would have a hard time even getting to Canada; some place closer would be better. Anyone you can stay with?"

"No, and I would not put them in jeopardy. If they come after me like they came after you . . ."

"Got it! Walnut Creek, I have an extra room. The place is comfortable; it's the least I can do. Do you like dogs?" The offer hung in the air waiting for an answer when Sharon's phone began to ring, no number.

"Sharon O'Mara."

"Having a nice lunch? Ms. Luca looks especially nice today and you must have done quite a bit of shopping."

Sharon wrote down "Pinkie" on the napkin and showed it to Luca. "You must try the calamari here; it's just wonderful and, by the way, how are your boys? Lucky, I guess—they should all be dead. We're busy with lunch, goodbye."

Evelyn Luca looked stunned. "You hung up on her."

"Of course. She is disturbing a business meeting and our

lunch, how rude. She knows we are here, must have followed you, or one of her people did. No big deal. If she wanted you dead, we would not be having this conversation. She needs you, for now. We need her to show her face."

"She knew your phone number!"

"She took it from the records in your shop; I don't like to change phone numbers. My guess is that her cell is a CVS special with minimal calling time, and then she throws it away. The Feds can't trace it. What about my offer? It's the least I can do after the major fuckup at the warehouse."

"I wasn't sure. I tend to be a private person, but now almost everything is laid out in the open. But she knows where you live, that's obvious."

"It's the last place she would go; she might even think there're cops around, watching the house. It's better than a hotel, maybe not the Four Seasons, but cheaper. And I'm not a bad cook."

"Ah, cooking. Some of my family were restaurant owners— why I didn't stay in the business, I still don't know. I can cook my way through just about anything you want, French, Italian, even a few good German dishes."

"Maybe this won't be a good idea; I love food too much. And, at my age, it's beginning to love me too much also. You, a little size two, and me and a plate of linguine vongole—Pinkie is less dangerous."

"Please, I work very hard to fit into this suit and I understand. It's also getting harder and harder, but I do want to live. I'll take your offer. I can also manage the store's reopening better if I'm closer."

Luca picked at the Calamari, but ordered another wine. Sharon ordered a Caesar salad; Luca passed. She let Luca stew a bit and then asked, "Your family, restaurants, handbags, leather goods?"

"My mother's family is in restaurants; my father's is in leather. They both run successful businesses and my brothers and sisters bounce back and forth between the two. I have always stayed on the fashion side."

"What do they think about all this?"

"They're not happy about it; this needs to be over so I can reopen. The Feds are waiting; I feel like bait. My guess, since Lau knows we are talking, without being able to get to me, she will turn to you. She may think there's more going on than what's really happening."

"I hope so; I will need information on your shipments and sources. Your handbags come from Italy . . ."

"Actually from outside Marseilles, but don't tell anyone. We get better work and our costs are less in France—hard to believe but true—and most of the craftsmen are from Hungary and Portugal. The handbags are flown to our stores around the world via Federal Express; it's more secure. But our family headquarters is in Florence."

"Love Florence. Spent three days on an R&R break when I was in Iraq. Gives you a greater understanding of time and the battles we fight: the Medici, Michelangelo, the great food. But it was all formed around wars and family feuds and rivalries, not much different today."

After they worked out the logistics, Sharon took BART back home. Luca, after picking up a few things, would meet her at her cottage. Luca promised her veal scallops with Marsala for dinner; Sharon pledged an excellent, but affordable, bottle of wine.

Chapter 9

The musty odor of tanned leather filled the early morning work floor like the smog that hung between the new apartment towers of Dongguan. Forty rows of sewing machines, like phalanxes of Mao's soldiers, stood at attention, each with a black-haired young girl hunched over the small space where a needle was driven through leather. When each piece was stitched and finished, it was set aside for the next in line to add another piece of the soft leather. The floor held hundreds of women, all dressed in a simple smock, all with short hair, all not daring to talk or look beyond their sewing machines. As the early light came through the windows, a whistle blew through the room and the small lights on the machines were clicked off to save electricity.

Deng Jiao hated this time of day. This was when you could not see; it would be almost an hour before the room would be light enough to properly sew. But the floor manager would not accept mistakes. She redoubled her efforts to be careful, to make the stitches the way she was shown, to be very careful, trying not to run the needle through her finger, and to make sure she would not be singled out for discipline. It had been a long year and a half since she left the mountains, and now, with her cousin's disappearance, she was alone.

"You must go with this man, Jiao. There's nothing here; he has a job in Dongguan for you. I have no food and I have my own family to care for. You must go."

"Yes, Uncle," Jiao said, tears streaming down her cheeks. "I will go. Is Mei going also?"

"Yes, she also has a job working in the same factory as you; you will be together. You can take care of yourselves now," her uncle said, as he sipped on a small bowl of tea. She never learned what he'd been paid for them.

Deng Jiao and Deng Mai found each other two hours after the earthquake leveled their small village of Beichuan in the mountains of Sichuan. They clung to each other, hoping that the pile of rubble and shattered concrete would release their parents still alive. But after three days, they were sure that they were dead. No one had come to help them move the concrete, and none would respond to their calls for help. Now they were alone, single children, orphans with only each other for company. Some food was offered from a cart pushed through the town by a city official; his family was also gone. All he had was the cart. A small doll that had been his daughter's sat on the countertop. He offered a thin gruel of rice and chicken stock to those in need.

"We have been told the road will be open in two days and then we will have food and help. Are you girls alright?"

"Yes, Uncle. We'll be okay; we have a dry place to sleep and towels to cover our faces. Two days, you said?" Mei asked.

"Yes, two days, then maybe we can find the others and lay them to rest."

Everyone was related in this village. Their uncle had walked up the hill from the large pit containing hundreds of his friends and relatives. All crushed by the massive quake. The school building still held hundreds of their classmates not recovered. Jiao knew his wife and daughter were buried in the large pit with cousins and great uncles, all crushed by stone and concrete. She learned that he had been walking along the river when the earth rolled and threw him to the ground; his need to smoke was all that saved him.

Deng Jiao and Deng Mei had left the school early to help at home. There was to be a party that evening for their great-aunt, who was turning eighty years old, and their mothers asked permission for the girls to leave and help. All were dead: mothers, fathers, their great-aunt, the school's principal and students. They stood huddled together in the middle of the street, while their world collapsed around them.

Now, two days later, the mountains continued to shake

and they seldom slept for more than an hour. They never left each other's side; they held hands in the makeshift latrines built along the river. They slept curled against each other. There was nothing left for them in Beichuan.

"How do you know this man, Uncle?" Mei asked.

"I have done business with him in Chengdu; he works with some of the biggest companies in Guangdong and Dongguan. He is an important man. He finds work for people, good work with good pay."

To the girls, Guangdong was on the far side of the world. They had read about the city in their magazines and saw the TV shows. But it was a world apart, a place where people they knew from the village went to and never returned. Their parents received a few letters, then none. A great-uncle said the world was falling apart, and now, after the earthquake, Mei was sure that it was true.

As promised, in two days, the road was opened and emergency relief poured into the valley. Large earthmoving equipment passed through the village into the mountains where the river had been dammed by landslides. If not cleared, even more death would wash through what remained of the towns along the river.

The two cousins, their uncle, and three other orphaned girls stood together in a cleared parking lot near the large tent with a sign: "Headquarters for the Relief Effort." A soldier stood nearby. Each girl had a small drawstring bag that held everything they owned; they both wore heavy coats. The uncle smoked one cigarette after another. He hesitated for a moment before lighting another.

A small van appeared from down the road and turned into the parking lot; the smoke from the muffler choked the clean air. Two men walked toward the small group, and the uncle moved forward, the cigarette hanging loosely from his lips. Mei and Jiao watched as they shook hands and talked quietly. The uncle waved the girls over.

"This is Mr. Chu; he will be taking you to Chengdu. From

there, this man, Mr. Lee, will escort you to Dongguan on the train."

The girls all looked at each other. None had ever been on a train; none had been out of this valley. Numb, they all nodded to the strangers. The smallest, who Mei thought could not be more than thirteen, began to cry. Jiao looked closely at Lee, broad shoulders, hard eyes, short-cut hair, and dark gray tee shirt—at least it was clean. She also noticed the tattoos on his arms; a dragon coursed its way down the right arm to encircle a single character. She shivered. It said, "Blood."

As they came down, they passed hundreds of trucks towing large trailers with earthmoving equipment and bulldozers heading back up into the mountain. Even the dump trucks held smaller backhoes and other large strange-looking tools. They were not stopped at any of the checkpoints and were waved on as they passed. The two men smoked continuously.

The land flattened to farmland with hundreds of small garden plots and stone homes along the four-lane asphalt road. Many of the homes had collapsed roofs and their walls had fallen over; the earthquake had rolled through this region as well. People sat on the front steps, cooking and making tea. The sun stood high over the road as they passed through the largest city the pair had ever seen, Deyang. Again they passed more trucks heading into the mountains. Two hours later, they arrived in Chengdu. To all the girls, this medium-sized town, by China's standards, was beyond their imagination. Tall apartment towers lined the streets; they were taller than the mountains that enclosed Beichuan. There were more people than they had ever seen and the river was lined with shops and great stores that they had only read about in magazines. The two men said nothing as they inched through the traffic. Lee finally turned to the girls, and said they would be at the train station in twenty minutes. The girls pressed their faces to the windows of the van and stared in wonder.

"Can we stop and look around? I saw a store I've always wanted to shop in," a girl asked.

"No, there will be plenty of time when you reach Donggu-an," Hong said. Jiao remembered later that this was the first of the hundreds of lies they were told.

"The train leaves in one hour and it's a long trip, almost two days," Hong said, when they reached the station. The girls looked at each other—all were surprised. "You will need food and something to drink. There are market stalls over there. Lee will give you money. He will go with you. I will buy your tickets; we meet back here in thirty minutes. Don't leave Lee's side; there are dangerous people here. Stay close to him, he will keep you safe." This was lie number two.

Jiao and Mei held hands and followed Lee and the others. The wonder of everything surrounding them was beyond their country upbringing, yet nothing prepared them for the size of the train station.

"Mei, I have never been in a building this big; there are pigeons in the rafters, and look at the windows—they look almost green."

"Yes, Jiao, but we need to stay close to Lee; you know what the other man said." Mei looked at Lee's back and at his arms; she was not sure why they needed to stay close to him. Her first instinct was to flee.

The trains were the most modern things the girls had ever seen, sleek and comfortable. The countryside slipped past in flashes of green and gray by the hundreds of kilometers. At Huaihua and at Guigang, they were joined by eight more girls; each group had their own escort. *They are meaner and harder looking than Lee*, Mei thought. These young girls looked more urban, tougher around the eyes; one kept falling asleep and had to be awakened by her escort. He was not nice about it.

The cities grew larger and the open countryside between the cities decreased. Huge towers filled the windows and were gone. They left the train only once and were reminded not to talk with anyone. Then they were hustled across the platform to a string of timeworn older cars and arrived at the Dongguan train station early in the morning. The city's morning air stank with a thousand odors the cousins had never smelled. This was not the clean air of the mountains; it stank like the millions of people that caused it.

9b

For a week, Mei watched the sun rise and set through the high glass windows. At least there was sunlight. For more than three weeks, there was nothing but rolling and rocking back and forth, and when the batteries died—only blackness. She and the other girls were sick the first few days, and finally, when their stomachs quieted down, the monotony began. The girls played games and talked. One started to cry and would not stop until she fell asleep. When she awoke, she started to cry again. They watched their water and food. The small corner set aside with a toilet and basin had long since become unusable; they survived by climbing into their souls and slowly retreating from the others. Mei remembered a vague banging and clanking then swaying; she tried to stand and then fell onto the filth that covered the floor. Then there was silence. Small vents, hidden along the top of the box, let in the dimmest of light. As she lay on her cot, she remembered that the meager daylight went on and off six times; they never moved. For Deng Mei, time had stopped and she was sure that her life was to end in this huge coffin with the other girls. The crying girl didn't move anymore.

A banging brought her back to reality; sunlight exploded into the coffin. Voices, men's voices, filled the box. A siren could be heard. She felt herself being carried, set on a soft bed, then nothing. A soft light again crept into the corners of her closed eyes; she heard voices, Chinese voices. Mei slowly turned her head toward the sounds. A woman's face materialized.

"Are you feeling better?" the face asked; her Chinese had a strange accent that was hard to understand. Mei nodded.

"Good, I'm Doris. We're nursing you back to health. It was wrong for them to have locked you in that box, but you're in good hands now. Understand?"

Again a nod. "Where?"

"You're in America and safe now. You're Deng Mei, correct?"

Again Mei nodded. "America?" *The moon is closer,* she thought. "Why America, why?" Mei mumbled.

"We will take care of you, then, when you are better, we can talk. There's much you can do to help us here. Go back to sleep and there will be dumplings and tea when you awaken."

Mei's eyes slowly closed, and she drifted asleep.

That was a week ago and now she was more afraid than when the earthquake crushed her village. Now she stood naked in front of a screen and she could hear men's voices; Chinese and another language that she thought might be English but could not understand. But the Chinese terms of "nice ass and legs" shocked her, and a hand on her leg made her jerk away from the touch. In the bright light she could see nothing.

"Hold still and don't move. Anyone move and I will strike the bottoms of your feet. Don't move." The voice was familiar but she could not remember, but a man's voice, when the coffin was opened, came back to her. She stood very still as more hands ran over her legs and body; she started shaking.

"Okay, that's enough for now; more later, gentlemen. Much more."

"You promised a good time, Hong. That's the third time you pulled me up short."

"And it won't be the last time, but you're a good customer so you get to see the new girls first. Now go. Alice is waiting in the last room. Go."

Deng Mei kept shaking, not sure what was going on.

"You'll get over it, sister, and in time you may even like it. But for right now, I own you. You want to live, you do as I say. You want to eat? Do as I say. If you want to pee, make sure you ask me first." Hong Feng led her back to the dormitory that confined her and the other girls. Four rows of bunk beds stuck out from the wall. Two of the original girls from the container were now gone, she didn't know where. One was from Huaihua, the one with hard eyes. She recovered faster than the others and understood what was coming. Mei still didn't understand. She missed her cousin.

A week later it was over, the terrible shock and the pain, the lightness in her head and that dreamlike feeling, and the rough man; now it was over. She cried for her loss and more from the fear of not knowing where she was. She had not seen the sky for two months. From the workshop and the sewing machines, to the apartment, then waking up in a van, and then again in the iron coffin, to recovery in this warehouse, she had never looked at the sun, the warm and glorious sun. She lay quietly on her bunk and thought of the mountains.

"You'll be alright, Mei. I got used to it, and now I don't think about it. It just happens," Jade said. "Just don't think about it; it will only make you sick. Me? I'm happy, good food and wine and a party once in a while, all good. Better than being with that asshole father of mine back in China. He was the first, you know, when I was fourteen, the bastard. So I took the first train I could get, got a job in Dongguan, changed my name, and here I am. I'm going to become an American someday."

Mei looked at Jade, and a tear coursed down her cheek. This was not what she imagined when her uncle said she would work in the big city for lots of money. Now she was alone, humiliated, and frightened. All she knew was that somehow she needed to get away from these people. The first face that she saw when she woke up had become the face of a witch.

"You're all invited to a party," Hong said. "Tonight you will all get new dresses, Western dresses and makeup and new hair-styles for a big party. These two ladies will help you dress and show you how to act."

Two extremely well-dressed Chinese women came into the room carrying bundles of black and red cloth. They set them on the table and one held up a dress. "Who wants this one?"

"Me, me." And the rush was on. Mei forgot, for a moment, why they were being given new dresses. She only remembered that they were so beautiful. Hers was a soft red silk dress with a small embroidered dragon on the shoulder. Makeup added color to her face. She stood at the mirror and wondered who the woman was that was looking back at her. Her weight loss had sharpened her cheeks and shoulders; her hair had grown out and was longer than allowed in the workshop. The lipstick, the first she had ever worn, tasted strange, but made her lips full. Even after the makeover, she was more afraid than ever. Where were they going?

The warehouse door opened and two large black limousines pulled into the open drive in the center of the concrete floor. Two sharply dressed Chinese men opened the doors for the six girls, three to each back seat. Mei sat against the door; she heard the door click after it closed. She tried the handle slowly as the cars moved out into the street, but it didn't move. Mei continued to stare out the window and watched the lights pass through the night; fog hung in the air, thick, like the fog back in Beichuan. These buildings were larger and stranger than the buildings she remembered in China. At a stoplight, she saw characters and signs all proclaiming food, liquor, and clothing. She shook her head. She could read these signs; they were in Chinese. She looked around and saw more—a billboard proclaimed a rock group she had heard of in China, in a magazine or something, again in Chinese. Finally a sign said "Oakland." What Oakland was, she didn't have any idea, but she guessed that it was where she was right now.

The cars went three more blocks and pulled up in front of a large apartment complex. The driver told the girls to wait. He would get back to them in a moment. Mei looked through the rear window and saw the other black car. The two drivers stood on the sidewalk talking; one had a cell phone to his ear. Mei suddenly remembered the small cell phone that her cousin, Jiao, had bought. It was one that she had to buy time for at the post office in order to use it; that way she didn't get a monthly bill. Small in size, the phone could easily be hidden from the factory manager. Cell phones were not permitted inside the factory, but all of the girls had one.

The driver approached the car and the doors clicked open.

"You can get out now," he said. "Go into the lobby and wait; you will be taken to the party from there."

As the drivers began to help the girls from the limousines, tires screeched from the intersection, and Mei turned to look. Three black SUVs headed straight for the group. Their windows were open and she saw chrome barrels pointing at the cars and at her. Explosions and more explosions came from everywhere. Mei stood frozen; Jade spun around while standing next to her, collapsed into her, then fell to the sidewalk. Mei felt wetness on her hands. One of the drivers managed to pull out his pistol and fired one round before he was hit and went down. Another girl screamed and fell. Then the other driver spun across the pavement and against the glass of the lobby window; more gunfire and the window exploded. Mei held her hands against her ears. The black SUVs turned the corner and disappeared, as quickly as they had arrived.

For five seconds, Mei looked at the carnage all around her. All the girls were on the ground. Three were still moving, one continued to scream, and Jade and another were twisted, their legs tucked wildly under them. The drivers lay where they fell; blood flowed down the sidewalk and met the small red streams continuing to pump from the girls.

Mei spun away from the gore and, as if possessed, ran up the hill toward the lights. One block, then another, then another, she ran. The uncomfortable heels twisted her feet so she kicked them off. She saw the only sign that made sense to her: "Norma's Tea House." She looked back down the street and turned into the bright lights of the tearoom.

* * *

Norma Chang looked up from reading her paper, and was stunned by the teenager that had just run into her small restaurant. Standing at the door, breathing heavily, stood a tall well-dressed Chinese girl, in a stunning red dress, bare feet, nice makeup, with blood on her hands and her right arm. Fear had replaced the makeup streaming down her face. Chang quickly stood, pulled the girl inside, slammed the door, and pulled the shades down. Her fifty-five years of living in Oakland gave her all the immediate and important information she needed.

"I need help," the girl said.

For the first time in Norma Chang's life, she heard Chinese as it was spoken in Shechuan, unadulterated, no slang, pure. Her heart skipped a beat.

"Are you all right, daughter, are you hurt?"

"No, I'm fine, but the others; there were guns and bullets, so I ran."

"Good, be calm, you're safe."

Sirens began to scream throughout the neighborhood. Red and blue lights flashed between the cracks in the shades.

"Were you involved in that?" Norma asked.

Mei shook her head. "They said we were going to a party; it was the first time I was outside in months. I got a new dress."

Norma had a very good idea about what was going on. She sat her down and poured Mei a cup of tea. "Are you okay?"

"I am now, mother, I am now." For the next hour, after telling Norma her name was Mei, she told her everything she could remember, every sordid detail that had happened to her. The coffin was the worst of it; Norma bit her lip as she listened.

"You sit here for a moment, I will be right back. Do you need anything?"

"No, I'm fine now, thank you." Mei sipped her tea; she had the look of a soldier in wartime, something Norma remembered from the final days of Vietnam working in the EVAC hospital.

Norma went to the back kitchen; she retrieved her cell phone and punched in a number.

"Danny, I need your help, I have a situation here. No, the shootings were a few blocks away . . . I thought you might be there . . . one of them is here, a frightened young girl. I`m surprised if she's all of sixteen . . . yes, see you shortly." Norma looked at the face of the young woman, and smiled. She was one of the lucky ones.

9c

The apartment was on the eighteenth floor and had three rooms: a small kitchen, a bathroom, and one bedroom. Four girls called the apartment their home. Deng Jiao and one girl had the day shift at the factory; the other two had the night shift. The four seldom saw each other for longer than an hour or two each week. At least they had their own cots and a small dresser to keep their things in. The one closet had been portioned into four parts with cardboard so that the girls could hang a few things. Her section held one coat and the one dress she had purchased. Half of her salary went to pay the rent; it was taken directly from her paycheck. The rest went for food, toiletries, the shared TV, and maybe a new blouse. She splurged every few months and bought makeup; the oldest girl showed her how to wear it.

Some of the girls were relieved when Deng Mei disappeared—there was more room in the apartment, but none told Jiao about their feelings. Jiao reported Mei's disappearance to the police. They seemed disinterested and annoyed.

"Sir, she would never leave and not tell me, we are like sisters. She would not leave and take nothing. I need to find her."

"Young lady, I'm sure she's just fine. Probably left with a boyfriend you didn't know about; she'll be back. That's always the way it goes," the policeman said.

She pleaded for an hour and the policeman finally took a report and said he would try and find out something. Three weeks later, there was still nothing to report. The girls at the factory told her about other girls that worked for a few weeks and then left. Jiao was told, "They disappeared, probably found a better job than this hellhole and moved on. Don't worry about Mei, she'll be back. Just wait. She will be rich and married. Just wait."

Deng Jiao was sure her cousin had not "just moved on." She kept her cell phone in her handbag. They were told at the factory that it was forbidden, but every girl she knew had one. She didn't flash hers around; only Mei knew she had a phone. One of the few benefits was that the small store sold defective handbags and other leather goods they worked on; to carry a bag that they could see in a magazine made them feel very special. The bag even had a small place where she could hide the phone. Since no one ever called her, and she had only given her number to her cousin, she was certain it would not ring and give her away. She left it off most of the time anyway.

After four weeks, Jiao was sure Deng Mei was dead. She had not run away with a boy, had not found another job, or even attempted to go home. Jiao's world became very small as she did her work, slept and ate in the cramped apartment, and, on her free day, walked to the large park not more than a mile from the complex.

The smoke and smoggy haze hung between the rows of high-rise apartments; when it rained it seemed the clouds just cried grey tears. The sun, crisp and sharp over the mountain in her village, was a bright disk of indiscernible light that hung in the jaundice-inflicted sky. From her perch on the park's hillside, she watched the city disappear along its edges in the yellow-gray gloom. Traffic bustled and honked incessantly below her. She didn't understand how the city could hold this many people and their cars. She could not afford a taxi or even the cost to share a ride with the girls, so she walked. Her world was defined by how far she could walk to and from a place on her day off.

She splurged this morning and bought a Coke and two pork buns from the cart near the apartment. They were never as good as the ones her mother made, but they did help her remember her family. She felt like a sword had cut her in two when she'd left the mountains and cut her again when Mei disappeared. Lovers and old people strolled the pathways and trails; even they needed a place to call their own in the chaos and clamor. They could hold their own small world in their hands here.

She rolled the phone in her hand; it was the most valuable thing she owned. The others, when they were out, would text each other messages and small bits about what they were doing, and send pictures to each other. She never understood all the fuss; why not just tell them face-to-face? She was too private a person to share her every moment with these chatterboxes. She pushed her thumb up and down the face of the phone, and her thoughts wandered to her lost family; she heaved a sigh and held her breath again, and slowly exhaled. She closed her eyes and hoped for silence; instead, her fingers suddenly started to shake and vibrate. The phone buzzed in her hand. Jiao dropped it onto her lap as if an electric wire had touched her. She stared at the device; it continued to vibrate.

"Hello?" Jiao said haltingly.

"Jiao, Jiao, is it you, Jiao?"

Deng Jiao, from Beichuan, with her phone to her ear, began to cry.

"Mei? Mei?"

9d

Nick Nethermann looked at the pictures spread across the table in front of him. Directly across sat Sergeant Danny Chang, and two others he didn't know; the redhead made him smile. She was cute, but in a tough sort of way; he couldn't put his finger on it. He knew Chang from the incident at the port with the girls and the follow-up with the Oakland PD. Good guy from everything he could see and very professional. He also took a great interest in the container and its missing cargo. All the girls were Chinese and this had a profound impact on Chang. Their conversations, even over the phone, told him that he would not give this up—ever. He wasn't sure why the others were at this meeting.

"Nick," Chang said. "This is Officer Kevin Bryan and Sharon O'Mara; they may have a link to this container's slave traders and some other port-related issues."

"Nice to meet you," Kevin and Sharon both responded together. They looked at each other and laughed. "We do that a lot," he said. "Swear we were married, at times."

Nick looked at the two and noted the strong comfort level between them.

"Nick, we had a break in the slave container thing, but before I go into it, I need you to look at these photos and see if you recognize anyone. I'll tell you more after," Chang said.

"Yes, sir. I understand," Nethermann said.

Chang laid two rows of photos on the table facing Nether-mann. The top row held five photos of women's faces; the second row held four men's faces. All were Chinese. Nethermann had seen mug shots before and two of the men had the usual front and side profiles. None of the women's were mug shots. In fact, one of the women looked suspiciously dead, a morgue shot. Nethermann looked at Chang.

"Yes, some of these people are dead."

Nethermann stared for a long minute; images flashed through his brain, like the spinning dials on a slot machine, then bells went off.

"These two." He pointed at the male photos on the right, the mug shots. "They were at the container and were the first two out of the EMT van. I had a good look at them before I was hit in the head; the man that did it isn't here. But I'm sure about the others."

He scanned the row of women. "This one—" he put his finger on the middle photo—"was one of the girls in the box. She was the first I went to and I gave her water; she could barely keep her head up. I remember her eyes; they were a mixture of relief and fear, like the kind I saw after a bombing in Iraq. Confusion, fear, total disorientation, like she didn't know who she was. She looks a lot better in this photo. Why?"

Chang told Nethermann about the girl, her escape, the shooting on the street, and how she found safety at his mother's teashop. Then he included Bryan and O'Mara in the conversation.

"Sergeant, these two were found dead on the sidewalk along with six girls that had been 'invited' to a party at the building." Chang pointed to the photos. "These two were killed, these two were injured, this one was lucky, and one escaped, the girl you pointed to. The survivors didn't know which apartment they were going to—our guess is that they were party favors for the guests and probably didn't know," Chang said. "We ran the

DNA on every one of these people. The girls had no papers or IDs; the men had driver's licenses that would pass muster, but were for people already dead. The DNA matched these two—" Chang pointed at two of the photos—"to blood found at a house shooting a few weeks back. It was Ms. O'Mara's house they shot up—Officer Bryan was also there. These two escaped. Obviously someone else caught up with them."

Nethermann looked at the woman. *Okay, I understand,* he thought, *but why is she here?*

O'Mara looked at Nethermann and smiled. "You're wondering why I'm here, Sergeant, I'll bet. Well, to be blunt, this is the third time these bastards have pushed their way into my comfortable little life. Once in Mexico with a container and four dead men hanging in it; the second was a warehouse and a container full of guns; and the last time was when they shot up my house and nearly killed my dog."

"What about me? I was nearly killed," Kevin offered.

"You're too tough to die," Sharon said, turning back to Nethermann. "I have a vested interest in this, and from what Danny said about the girl, this is a lot bigger than automatic weapons and knockoff handbags."

"Handbags?" Nethermann said, the confusion lifting. "You're the ex-Army cop that found that container in Mexico. Hell, ma'am, every Guardsman that works the port knows about that, wow. You think this girl is tied to that?"

"With a big ribbon, Sergeant," Kevin added. "Looks like these two fellows were the two that survived the shoot-out at the O'Mara corral, only to be shot up by someone else a few weeks later. The girl is a victim abducted from China for the sex slave racket here. These are all tied together: knockoff handbags, guns, and sex. It looks like we have a new group that's killing off members of another gang; this could be the start of a small international gang war."

"If so, I want to 'keep it in the family,' so to speak," Chang said. "I'm not happy about the shootings, but, for now, it seems to be between each other. Unfortunately, these girls didn't want to be a part of this. The girl that escaped told quite a tale of a promised job in the big city and eventually found herself here, pulling tricks for a pretty lady with a pink stripe in her hair. Her backup is a tall bald-headed guy. She told us everything she knew."

"That may be the guy that clocked me, fits his description: big, Chinese, and very bald," Nethermann added.

"Sergeant Chang, I object," Sharon jumped in. "They shot up my house and damn near killed my dog. Sounds a lot like not 'keeping it in the family' to me."

"I'm sorry, Sharon, you're right, but my concern is also here in Oakland where they do seem to keep it amongst themselves. I have also talked with San Francisco PD and brought them up to speed. ATF and Homeland are due here after lunch, just one big happy party. I hope I can keep some control over all this, before some federal agency waltzes in and really screws it up."

"Sir, I don't envy your job. And if I ever get that son of a bitch who clubbed me in my sights, he'll be real fucking sorry. Sorry, ma'am."

Sharon smiled. "Yes, Sergeant, and if I ever get to the god-damn fucking asshole that shot up my house and my dog, he'll wish he had stayed in China."

Nethermann smiled. "I like you, Lieutenant. Once Army, always Army."

* * *

Two hours before the meeting with Nethermann, Sharon and Kevin had stopped at Danny Chang's mother's house to see the girl. Sergeant Chang met them at the door.

"She is safer here than anywhere," Chang said. "Mom can talk with her, keep her calm. Her name is Deng Mei. She is surprisingly resilient. She is from the area crushed by that huge earthquake a few years ago—all her family was killed, been working in Dongguan at a leather plant. After about a year, she was asked to go on a date with a senior manager's son, very hush-hush, he said. The other girls would be envious. He also bought her a new dress; she's only seventeen. For these girls, any attention was better than the grind of the factory."

"Seventeen, good God, I can identify with that, no family, alone, lost," Sharon said. Kevin looked at her, another unknown bit.

"Not completely. Her cousin was also with her," Chang continued. "My guess, from what I've been hearing, their uncle, or some other relative, sold them to a man needing labor in the big city. These girls are from the backwoods, as we say here. Says she had never been out of the Beichuan Valley until she left with some other girls to go to Dongguan; they didn't even know where they were until someone at the factory told them. They were as lost as anyone could be. Most of the money promised to them went for rent and food; there was none to send home, even if they had someone to send it to."

"The cousin?" Sharon asked.

"Fascinating story. Mom and the girl were talking and Mom's phone rang. The girl jumped and then pointed at it. Seems her cousin also has a phone—maybe she can call her, tell her she's okay.

Mom checked with me and, after doing a little calculation with time zones and other things, like when she would be off work, they called. I'll tell you, the time zone thing and the fact that they're a day ahead really confuses me. So I just went with the info on my iPhone, time and day and all. She called and I'll be damned if the other girl, her name is Deng Jiao, didn't pick up. I thought I was in a room full of teenagers at my sister's house, all the squawking and jabbering, even Mom joined in. The girl kept talking and crying. My Chinese is rough, but I can deal with the people here. But Mom's smile got bigger and bigger as the two girls talked; it was something to see!"

The three entered the neat bungalow a few blocks from Lake Merritt; the stucco exterior was American craftsman. The interior was elegant Chinese from the chairs and wall pieces to the silk rugs. Norma Chang greeted them warmly, dressed in a comfortable outfit that could have come from a high-end Hong Kong department store, the perfect example of an elegant Chinese ma-tron. Sitting on the couch was a beautiful teenage girl, dressed in blue jeans and a Cal sweatshirt, her hair immaculate, her young face glowing.

Norma introduced everyone. Mei stood and, to Sharon's ob-vious surprise, Mei was tall. Even Kevin, all six-plus feet of him, was shocked.

Norma apparently noticed. "She is tall, especially for China, but they do grow them bigger in Sichuan. When Mei heard the word for her region, she smiled; she also looked at Sharon's red hair, and, after asking permission, ran her fingers through the long auburn tresses. She then ran her fingers through her own hair, and a conversation in Chinese started between Norma and Mei. Norma smiled, said a short word. Mei looked disappointed.

"I take it she wanted to change the color of her hair?" Sharon asked.

"She's still a teenager, even after all of this. Fashion is im-portant, even in China," Norma said.

Mei took in a gulp of air, pointed at Sharon's handbag, and started chattering. Norma and Mei went back and forth for at least a minute, and then stopped.

"This is very interesting, Sharon, my dear. Mei tells me she made that handbag you're carrying; it was one of the bags they spent two weeks making, many colors, but the green ones she made with her cousin, she's sure of it. Fascinating, isn't it, with this whole big world to shop in, she sees a handbag she made. She wants to know where you bought it."

Kevin and Sharon looked at each other. "I think you should hold off on that for now, don't you think?" He said. She nodded.

"Is this important?" Danny asked. "What's with the purse?"

"Handbag, Danny, handbag! Sharon, my dear, men—they just don't understand," Norma said, looking back and forth at the men.

"Yes, ma'am, they just don't have a clue, the little dears!"

"What?" Danny interjected. "What?"

On the way back to the station to meet with Nethermann,

Sharon brought Chang up to speed on Cabo San Lucas and the connections to the containers. He knew some of the overall gist of the story, but was fascinated by the details.

"Wow, this is getting more interesting and disturbing by the minute," was all he could add.

Chapter 10

10a

"**Are you sure** you don't want me with you during lunch? I could be there as a friend, you know, someone you just met, something . . ." Kevin said over the phone.

"Kevin, I said no!" Sharon added with emphasis. "No need. Inspector Lopez is a flirt and considers himself a ladies' man. My take, it's some of that Latin machismo thing. But he's harmless, and besides, I think he's kind of cute, in a gruff officer sort of way. He wouldn't screw up his meal ticket for a long weekend here in San Francisco and his all-expense-paid vacations to the US of A. The Feds would pull his passport in a minute if he did something stupid. And he's buying."

"Well, I'm concerned; call me when lunch is over, okay?"

"I will if I get the time, Dad!" Sharon said, emphasizing dad.

The Waterfront restaurant sits where Broadway dead-ends at the Bay—faulty car breaks and you buy everyone a round at the bar. After more than a quarter of a century, it still ranks as one of the best seafood houses on the Embarcadero. For a city wrapped on three sides by ocean and the Bay, there is an amazing lack of waterside seafood restaurants. Sure, some mention their views of the Bay, but very few can sit you at a window or on a deck where you look at seals, sailboats, and possible floaters. The Waterfront was one of the few; the Bay Bridge dominates the view to the south.

Just down from the Ferry Building and the farmers market, the restaurant was an easy ten-minute stroll from the Embarcadero BART station. Inspector Detective Xavier Lopez was nursing a beer when Sharon walked in.

"Señorita, it is an immense pleasure to see you again, and, most especially, at such a civilized venue such as this." The inspector stood and waved his arms about. He stopped, smiled, and took Sharon's hand in his, raised it, bowed, and, with a slight kiss, was done.

"And it's very good to see you, you look very well." Her bright complexion barely hid the blush on her cheeks.

"Si, very well, indeed. In fact, I have been given a slight promotion; I'm in charge of much of the drug investigations on the East Cape now, from La Paz to San Lucas. Dangerous these days, but since I'm one of the few who would take the job, and I have no family, the cartels can threaten all they want. I'm always in a position to shoot first and ask questions later." The last said with a great grin; Sharon had to laugh.

"A cocktail?"

"A little early for our usual, but I will have a glass of the Carmenet. Jose, the chardonnay, okay?"

The bartender smiled, but still looked at the large man with suspicion. Sharon went a long way back with this restaurant and if there was an issue he would be ready.

"And drop the serious face, Jose. Inspector Detective Lopez and I are old friends."

"Si, Señor. Sharon and I met over a pile of dead bodies," Lopez said, trying to impress the bartender.

"Pay him no mind, he exaggerates. There were only four."

Jose, eyes wide open, quickly opened a new bottle and poured a generous glass of the golden chardonnay; the aroma filled the air.

Lunch was simple, calamari and a salad; Lopez had the salmon, something he seldom had in Mexico. The bottle from the bar ended up on the table and now sat empty.

"Excellenté. Sharon, I enjoy this fish very much and it's very rare in Cabo San Lucas—but we have so much more kinds to eat, an excellent recommendation."

Sharon smiled. "You're here with the task force on this smuggling?"

"Yes. Our little adventure made the Federalies, both in Mexico and the United States, take notice. They want to understand how far this extends. The most we can see in Mexico is how the cartels are trying to take advantage of the Mexican ports and access to the northern US ports in LA, Oakland, and Seattle. From the little that gets out, there seems to be a war brewing between the Mexicans and the Chinese that use these ports as transfer locations; some of the Chinese goods have been found in Mexico City. We traced the containers to the port at Manzanillo and it was there that we think the four men were killed. They were all crew from the same ship that was carrying the container; all we can guess, at the moment, was that they were guarding something, and, when they would not give the information, they were killed. Or maybe they were killed to send a message up here. You, finding the box, ensured that the message was not received."

"That can work up to a point, Xavier; other boxes in the same shipment did arrive and we're fairly certain they were full of guns and other knockoff goods. One box, from another manifest, was full of young teenage Chinese girls destined for the sex trade here."

"Madre Dios, they're worse than scum, but I can see why the cartels are interested. Drugs and guns are one thing, but young women are an up-and-coming commodity for these people. These are things that, even in Mexico, are not tolerated. The cartels see competition from these Chinese gangs. They don't accept that they move the containers through their ports on the way to the United States," Lopez said. "They see it as a logical extension of their own business interests. Besides, you can create an income stream from thirteen-year-old girls. Once you put drugs up your nose, they're gone and you need to find more drugs."

"From what I hear, they're hardly keeping a low profile in Mexico with headless bodies all over the place."

"Si, but they are making a big mistake now, killing the politicians, even though many may warrant that action. The politicians are increasing the pressure on these groups, and my guess is they don't want the competition and may even be moving into the same rackets. But the Chinese can get guns and other armaments. These are things the cartels need. So the devils make bargains, may they all go to hell." Lopez pulled out his cigar case and extracted a large Cohiba.

"Xavier, not here; there're laws, you know."

"I will wait, but you Americans confuse me. You want to outlaw a perfectly excellent habit, with fine properties for thinking and conversation, and make legal a stupid plant that muddies the mind and results in hundreds dying each week in my country to supply the weed. Yes, we are a confusing people, are we not?" Lopez held up his glass and saluted the window and the Bay.

"Yes, Xavier. Humans are a nasty lot," she said, and added her glass.

Lopez lit her Marlboro as they stood at the rail overlooking the Bay. He finally ignited his cigar and blew a soft haze into the gentle breeze.

"I'm in meetings tomorrow and the next day. May I have the pleasure of another date, maybe dinner one of these evenings?"

"Possibly, but there are some interesting things happening and I believe I'll be in some of those meetings, so let's see what happens."

They finished their tobaccos. Xavier kissed Sharon on both cheeks. He strolled up the Embarcadero toward Fisherman's Wharf; she took BART back to Walnut Creek.

10b

"Who the hell shot up the apartment building, Fang? Who?" Doris Lau screamed, her cheeks nearly matching the slash of color in her hair. "We lost two men and six girls, and now the police have at least two of the girls, alive. They can't say much but they know my face and yours."

"It has to be the Manzanillo cartel—only they would be bold enough to do this. I have heard, through the port, that the one box that didn't arrive held four bodies as a present for us. They were missing from the ship after it left Manzanillo; obviously they were killed and put in the box to frighten us, to scare us

off. I will never be frightened by an ignorant gang of Mexicans,"
Hong Fang said.

"That may be, but I'm more concerned over the loss of the
income those girls would have produced, as well as the expense
to get them here, all gone. The games these Mexicans play are an
annoyance; but how are they finding out about our shipments
and cargos? That's the big question. It's one thing to kill our
people; it's another to know where and when they'll be there."
Lau threw a stack of papers across the floor; Fang stepped aside
as they flew in his direction.

"And it's your fault; you're supposed to be head of security
and protection for the family here. This should never have happened. No one should have known about the party, no one. Yet
an SUV pulls up and blasts some of my best girls to hell. I don't
give a goddamn fuck whether it was Manzanillo or the Italian
fucking Mafia, how did they know? Find out; do what it takes,
but find out."

"I lost two men," Fang protested.

"They were fucking overhead and they fucked up that
shooting in Walnut Creek. Those girls are the reason why you
can afford to drive that stupid black Mercedes you have; they
are the reason for us being here. Get it? Get the hell out, you
won't find answers here. They are out there."

Doris Lau, since the warehouse shooting, had lain low. She
had been chased by phone calls from China and LA, constant-
ly, all demanding updates about the warehouse being compro-
mised. There was even one call from Italy; she could barely
understand the conversation, but she understood the meaning:
"Find out what the hell happened."

Fifteen years had passed since her immigrant father told her
about the business. His small trinket shop on North Broadway,
in downtown Los Angeles, was a conduit for goods from China
to the United States. Los Angeles Chinese wanted many things
from their home country that were not permitted in the United
States: opium, special herbs, duty-free materials, and relatives,
especially relatives. It was lucrative but it required more than a

thuggish mentality to run the operation. When Doris Lau graduated from USC, a short three miles from her father's market, with a business degree, she spent a year in Dongguan and other parts of China, perfecting her Chinese and understanding the scope of the ancestral family's business interests. They were on all continents, in all the major cities of the world, and through interests, legal and illegal, involved in both politics and commerce control. If there were a Fortune 100 for gangsters, they would have ranked close to the top. But one thing was strictly enforced: secrecy. Even their ancestral family name was forbidden to be spoken outside of China; the tattoo was a symbol, like a business card. It also didn't hurt to have military connections in the China army to ease the paperwork and gain access to certain goods and transportation facilities. Few knew, but Lau did, that the family controlled the PCL container shipping company.

Lau's master's thesis was on franchises. This was how she looked at the family. It was an international collection of regional businesses that looked at the specific market they were in, found out what was needed, and then supplied it. Like a hamburger chain, when the desires of their customers change, so do their business models. What was in demand at one time, opium, was now replaced by higher-grade heroin and cocaine. What was once only relatives were now Chinese girls. All were commodities to be managed and profited from.

The family business continually rubbed against opposing interests. The heroin came from Thailand and Burma and even Afghanistan; the arms from the "excess" of the military suppliers in China; the girls from a never-ending supply of young unwanted women produced by 1.3 billion people. A few hundred, even a few thousand, girls were not going to be missed. Unfortunately, for the family, the growers of opium poppies and South American coca were becoming better organized; they were sending their children to universities and were becoming business competitors. Lau wondered what Burger King and McDonald's would be like if they played by the rules of the cartels and the family with their body dumps in parking lots. And Burger King did not kill the franchisee if they fucked up.

During the past two days, Deng Mei never showed herself at any place where Lau had spies in the alleys of Oakland's Chinatown. She could be dead and lying on a slab in Oakland's morgue, that was the next place to check. Maybe a bullet got her and it just took time for her body to show up. Lau would find out. Until then, the other girls had to be kept quiet, and off the street; she could not afford to lose any more of them. To keep them quiet required trinkets and sparkly things, cheap at any price.

She also stayed off the streets; if it was the cartel gunning for them, there was no sense becoming a target. There were preparations to make in order to receive the next shipments and the required clearance paperwork to complete at the port. These boxes were not going anywhere near Mexico—that stop was eliminated. Lau was pissed that the executions of her people did what they were intended to do: forced them to stay away from Mexico. After a long conversation with her cousin, who ran the Mexico City operation, he also decided to strengthen his defenses and bring in more people. For now, all seemed quiet, even for events that were now over a month old. The Mexican franchise worked as a go-between for the heroin trades in the New World and the Far East. Never a competitor, they acted as the logistics manager—boxes arrived, goods were transferred, small fees were paid. It worked well and had done so since the end of World War II, when the family was one of the first to go back into the mountainous areas of Southeast Asia after the Japanese were destroyed. Commerce hates a vacuum.

10c

"Sergeant, it's good that you're okay; not sure what I would do if one of your Guardsmen were injured or even killed on my docks. This isn't the port of a hundred years ago and the Barbary Coast." Thaddeus Spinos stood and shook Nick Nethermann's hand as the big National Guardsman walked into his office; Nethermann didn't need an escort like civilians. "Sit, sit.

Coffee?"

"Thank you, Mr. Spinos, yes, black, thanks," Nick said.

"Gloria, could you bring the sergeant a cup of coffee? Thanks." Spinos turned. "Should be good. We have an arrangement with one of the regional coffee companies that bring a couple of hundred million pounds of coffee through the port each year, good stuff." Spinos slid into his chair and adjusted a few papers. "Now, what can I help you with?"

"Mr. Spinos, I'm trying to find out why the box I was looking for was lost. I know there're thousands out there, but my logistics training and work, both here and Afghanistan, keeps me up to date on the latest tracking systems. This box seemed to fall through the cracks, almost as if on purpose. We found very little information on the box to help us find out what was supposed to be inside it and the path it took from China to Oakland. The evidence is all there, but China is a big ticket to America. Where it came from in China and where it was delivered to in America is another matter. My superiors are trying to piece it all together, but whoever pulled this off is good, real good. Their timeliness and this sore chin—" Nethermann rubbed his face—"attest to their vast knowledge of the port."

"I agree. I have over two thousand people coming and going in this port daily; it's very hard to ensure their credentials every time they enter. There definitely seems to be someone who knows a lot about how this place runs. With the millions of containers coming and going, it looks like they rely on the dark spots between the surveillance systems to get their boxes out. Legit paperwork, the right RFIDs, and changing trucking companies often helps a lot. I'm trying to drill down through all the paperwork and see if there's a system in place here. Hell, Homeland has been all over the port and me since then; I know it's not because of the cargo. They're more concerned about those containers that go boom, big booms. Me, I'm more concerned about making sure this place isn't shut down." Spinos walked to the window.

"Good coffee, Mr. Spinos. Very good; I may even change

brands because of it," Nethermann said, blowing on the cup's rim. "I understand the box's RFID was not the same one that might have left China."

"That's one possibility. We received the readouts from Guangdong—that's where the boxes came from; there were four on the manifest, as we've found out. Some of the paperwork suggested that there were only three, and when three arrived, no worries. One may have fallen off the ship in a storm off Mexico after it left Manzanillo, it never arrived here; that may have been the one that that woman O'Mara found. Two were delivered to a warehouse in San Francisco, the ones O'Mara discovered, her again. She's like a dog with a bone. And the one that you and your men found here was the lost one. God knows how many others may have passed through here under a similar intentional mix-up. The ones in the San Francisco warehouse didn't match up; looks like the numbers were switched." Spinos squinted into the sunlit port's yard; stacks of multi-colored boxes filled the horizon from one edge to the other. Large cranes, like the walking giants in a Star Wars movie, dominated the skyline. The hills and towers of San Francisco stood as a backdrop to the Bay Bridge and the port.

Nethermann nodded; he knew all this. But, for now, the Oakland PD asked that he not tell anyone about the girl. He understood; things were not much different in the Guard—keep info to yourself until needed.

"Yes, that O'Mara woman does keep showing up. Never met her; someone said she's ex-military." Nethermann looked over the coffee cup, trying to spot a reaction.

"Really? Didn't know. She stopped by here to find out more about the shipments and the workings of the port. Cute, in a sort of hard-edged way. She found the San Francisco boxes a few days after I saw her, then all hell broke out for a week, with the Feds and everyone all over my records. We came out well; that's the way I run things here. I'm not responsible for what's in the damn things, only that they get in and out of here as fast as possible." Spinos pointed his fist across the yard. Nethermann noticed a flash of red beneath the rolled-up sleeve of his white shirt—it was the corner of a red tattoo; he didn't see more, as Spinos lowered his arm.

"I fully understand," Nethermann said. "My fellows and I are heading south for a few weeks to help along the border. Would it be too much bother for you to send me an update now and then if something comes up? I will be so far in the boonies that even my mother won't know where I am. But we have email!"

"Sure, Sergeant, sure. Glad to. You guys have been a great help here and that's the least I can do. Should not be a security problem. I'll let you know what happens, if anything." Spinos shook Nethermann's hand and walked him to the door.

"Thanks, Mr. Spinos; thanks, and thanks for the coffee." Nethermann walked down the hall to the foyer. He didn't need to turn around to see Spinos's eyes following him. He knew they were there and now the man was very suspicious. Good, that's the way they wanted it.

Chapter 11

"**You didn't tell anyone**, did you, Jiao? Please tell me you didn't tell that blabbermouth Huan; you didn't say anything, did you?" Mei said into the cell phone. Norma listened to the conversation.

"No, Mei, I didn't. I know what they are now and after what they did to you, I won't tell a soul. Do you think they're looking for you?"

"Mrs. Chang says they are; there's talk on the street. I stay here in the house. It's such a wonderful house, you should see it. Everyone is so nice. I have new clothes, and it's funny, Jiao, the labels all say *Made in China*. I come so far and everything is from home. I do wish for Mom's pork buns. Mrs. Chang makes very good buns but not as good as Mother's." Norma looked at the girl with a slight frown; Mei cocked her head, as only a teenager could, and smiled.

"When you told me about the handbags, I wondered about that for days," Jiao said. "How it got there and why that woman had it? I still think about it. You remember how we helped to box them up and load the cartons into that big red shipping container? The fellow on the dock, you know the good-looking muscular fellow from Hong Kong, kept talking to you. It was the only container of handbags that were that color along with the orange ones, I think. Remember?"

"Yes, Jiao. You're right! It was that container. He was kind of cute, wasn't he? The others were scum; I bet a couple of them couldn't even read and write and the Hong Kong fellow did all the writing. Remember how he was on the phone all the time when he wasn't flirting?" Mei said.

"He asked me out."

"Who did?"

"The Hong Kong fellow. He saw me after work, leaving the factory; he walked up casually and started a conversation. He is very nice, and he is cute. His name is Kang; I don't know the family name. We had some tea from that cart by the park. He was very proper, and did I say he was cute?"

"Yes, Jiao, you did. Why did he ask you out?" Mei was getting suspicious. Norma moved closer to Mei, a question on her face.

"Because he said I'm one of the prettiest girls in the factory," Jiao answered. "And he wanted to know more about me. He was very respectful, Mei. He was, really. And he asked about you. Of course, I didn't say anything, only that you had disappeared and I didn't know where you were."

"Why would he ask about me? I only saw him a couple of times."

"Don't know. He asked about home and the earthquake and other things. He asked if I had a phone so he could call me. I'm no country girl now, Mei. I said I'm saving all my money for a new dress and that I have no time for all the phone silliness. He laughed and said all girls are the same, only concerned about clothes and makeup."

"Where are you now?"

"It's a beautiful day and I'm in the back of the park. Lots of people walking around; I'm on that bench where we used to sit and eat Sunday lunch. I don't think anyone followed me."

"Jiao, be very careful. After everything that's happened to me, I don't trust anyone, and neither should you. Make sure that your phone can't be found; they can find out where I am if they find your phone. I don't think you should see the Hong Kong guy; he is dangerous, I think."

"I understand, but he's so cute. By the way, we are making those handbags again. A little different, more spangles and rings, very nice leather and in different colors. The label is the same, STIA. But we're having trouble getting the studs to stay on the leather, very difficult work. The floor manager says that we need to make them work, so they asked for my advice. Mei, they asked for my help. I couldn't believe it."

"The red-haired woman, Sharon, says they're fake. The real ones are made somewhere in Europe, wherever that is. I didn't understand what she meant when she said fake. Mrs. Chang said they were duplicates of someone else's designs. Still don't understand, but I guess it's illegal or something."

"Mei, they're not fake. They're real bags and it's nice to work with the leather, it's so soft. I saw the beautiful drawings they use to make the patterns, but I couldn't read the letters—they were in another language. So I don't know what she's talking about. We are making hundreds every day; they're being boxed up as we finish them. They're large red containers in the shipping yard like last time; the cardboard boxes are going into them. I asked Kang and he says they're supposed to be out of here next week. I don't know where they're going. Should I find out?"

"Just a minute, Jiao." Mei turned to Norma and told her what Jiao had said. Norma put her finger up and punched in a number on her cell phone. Mei had been talking to Jiao on the house phone; it was cheaper.

"Danny, I need to ask you a few things; seems we have interesting things brewing in China."

11b

Sharon sat across the room from Deng Mei and Norma Chang. Danny Chang sat between them like a referee.

"Mom, tell Sharon what you found out."

"Well, it's all so surprising. Sharon, dear, as you know, Mei's cousin still works at the factory where they made the handbags. Deng Jiao is her name. They have been on the phone a lot and jabbering about this and that. My biggest fear is that she might get caught by the thugs that run the factory; my professional guess is that they have connections to the slave ring that brought Mei here. Danny, we need to try and get that girl out of there, I'm very concerned." Norma looked at her son; he nodded.

"Anyway, Jiao is making handbags again with the same brand as yours, STIA. Danny mentioned that you were involved

with the real company that makes those bags. They're love-
ly, dear, they really are, but, on my little teashop's profits, my
handbags only come from the discount table at Macy's, but we
women do love our bags. I probably have—"

"Mother, back to the point."

"Oh, yes, Jiao. Seems the girl is involved fixing some construction problems with the new bags, and she saw some plans
they have at the factory. They were plans for the patterns and
metal pieces, something about small metal studs and their locations. Jiao says the plans are in a language she can't read. That's
no surprise, but they do have the same logo, like the one on your
bag, at the top: *STIA* in large letters. I'm just an old foolish woman but I think that those plans may be the same ones from the
design house in Italy, maybe stolen or sold and being used to
make the fakes."

Sharon smiled. "That's a good deduction, Mrs. Chang. Very
good. I guess having a cop for a son does rub off."

"Actually two cops—Danny and his father, Captain Lee
Chang; lost him a few years ago to cancer. I taught both men
a lot about police work and I'm proud of them both." Norma
smiled at her son; Danny turned a bit red from the praise.

Sharon smiled at Danny. "See, you do need to have a woman around. Where would you be without her?"

"Let's move on, okay, Mother?"

"Sharon, here's the thought. I know you're trying to help
the company by finding out where the counterfeiters get their
information. Maybe I can get Jiao to snap a photo or two of the
plans next time she is alone and send them to us. You check out
the photos and maybe your client can track back to where the
plans came from, then you have them."

"There's no way I can put that girl in jeopardy; it's just not
right. These people don't give a damn about these girls, and if
she were caught, who knows what they would do. I think we
need to find another way," she said.

"I asked Jiao about it; she said that, after what they did to
Mei, there's nothing she would like to do more. Maybe these

people can be shut down if it can be proven that they stole the designs. They raise them right in the mountains around Beichuan." At the name of her village, Mei smiled at Norma, almost like she knew what was being said.

"What can I say, Norma. It scares the hell out of me, but I guess, if these people aren't stopped, who knows how many others face the same fate as Mei. It's not really my call; it has more to do with Jiao and you. Whatever I can do, let me know; I'm going to delay telling the STIA people about this for the moment; I'm not sure what ears are listening when Evelyn Luca calls home. When will this happen?"

"Mei talked to Jiao early this morning; it was early evening in Dongguan. Jiao thinks there's a chance for her to take photos tomorrow. Jiao will send the photos as soon as she's safe, probably after work, so maybe tomorrow morning."

"That fast?"

"Mei says the room with the drawings is just off the main floor. There are two men who work in the room, and they take long lunches and drink a lot. While they're out, maybe she can get a picture using a ruse; she may just have to look at the fittings. I told her that it's better to ask permission than to sneak in. She sounds like a bright young woman; both of these girls would make their mothers proud."

11c

Deng Jiao never left her machine all morning; the floor boss passed by twice and complimented her on her work; he seldom did that. She mentioned the continued difficulty with the studs and their mounting; on the second pass, he suggested she check the drawings again. Jiao looked at the office across the floor. The two men stood in the door, smoking. After a five beat, they crushed their cigarettes on the floor and started to walk toward the exit at the far end of the factory. Jiao passed them, only stopping to ask the taller man if she could look at the drawings to figure out how the studs were placed.

"Sure, Jiao, go ahead, no problem. By the way, when are you

going to accept my offer for dinner?"

"Mr. Chow, you are married and I don't date married men."

"I told you, Fang, she'd shut you down. Let's see, now you owe me . . ."

"Shut up, Chu. Go ahead, Jiao, but keep an open mind. There's always the chance of a promotion."

"Yes, sir, thank you, sir."

Jiao quickly walked toward the office and pushed the squeaky door open. The plans were laid out on the large table; paper and cardboard shapes littered the tables and the floor. She pushed the door closed behind her and left it open, just a crack. Trying not to look too suspicious, but not acting slowly, Jiao retrieved the phone from her pocket, held it over the plans, and snapped two pictures; she also took a couple of the next plan. She slid the phone back into her pocket; the door squeaked open.

"What are you doing here, Jiao?"

Jiao froze; she knew the voice all too well. "Kang, I'm looking at the plans to figure out a problem. Mr. Chow said it was okay." She turned and looked at Kang. "And besides, what are you doing here? You're not supposed to be inside on the floor."

"Why I'm here isn't your business, and besides, the real reason I'm here is to ask you to have tea with me."

"Tea?" Jiao tried to cut the conversation short and get back to her sewing machine. There were a hundred girls waiting for anyone working at the factory to make the first mistake. The floor manager, even though he told her to check the plans, also wanted his own quota met.

"I'm going for tea after work, care to join me?"

"Can't. I have to wash my hair." It was the first excuse that came to mind.

"Your hair looks wonderful. Come on, just some tea and a few cookies. What could that hurt? Besides, I like your company and you can tell me more about the mountains—never seen them myself." Kang continued to press.

"Kang, I really can't. Not tonight."

"It's just my brother and me; he's asked Huan, your roommate. She said yes, so I can't be a third wheel. Just some tea. You'll be home by eight. Plenty of time to wash your hair then," Kang persisted.

If Huan was going, maybe it would be okay even if she couldn't keep her mouth shut for a minute. Maybe the boys would get tired of listening to her and she could get home early. Jiao relented. "Okay, but just tea."

"Excellent. It's supposed to be chilly, so maybe you should wear a coat," Kang added.

"Coat? Oh, alright." She had a locker at the factory for some personal things, things she could afford to lose in case someone broke into it. Her apartment closet space was so small that this locker acted as an extension. The coat was one of the few things she brought from the mountains.

Huan was happy when she learned that they were double-dating.

"It'll be so much fun; those boys have money, lots of money. And they know how to show a good time to a country girl. Yes, they do. Last time we had tea, then a movie, then dinner, and all he wanted was a quick kiss. In fact, I had to encourage him to even do that. Yes, he's cute and even shy. Can you believe it? I had to encourage a kiss from him. Really, Jiao, isn't that just too funny?"

"Yes, Huan, it's just too funny." In Jiao's eye, Huan was just a bit above average, soft full face, long hair, not tall, average height. But when she took off her cheap glasses, her eyes dominated her face and, to Jiao, they were gorgeous. But, by the grace of the moon, that girl could talk a politician into his grave.

They completed the last of the handbags; today they were an amazing color—burnished gold. The leather looked like metal, but the feel was like holding a soft pillow filled with goose down. She stitched the last bag and secured the last ring to the shoulder strap; she timed it with the claxon sounding the end of the shift. She turned to the girl standing behind her waiting to take her stool.

"See you tomorrow," Jiao said.

"Tomorrow, Jiao, tomorrow." The girl was new and still trying to get used to the regimen; she looked tired.

Jiao met Huan in the locker room; it was obvious that Huan had bolted into the room at the sound of the horn. Makeup brightened her face from ear to ear, bold earrings hung from each lobe. She had replaced her smock with a bright dress and added comfortable shoes. "Come on, slow poke, the boys are waiting."

Jiao slid into the small bathroom and shut the door. The toilet was the old style, just a hole in the floor, but at least it was private. She quickly moved the pictures on her phone, checked the signal, dialed, and waited . . . ten seconds passed, then twenty.

"You coming, Jiao? Come on, it can't take that long to pee."

Jiao watched the phone; finally it said the transfer was done. She closed the cover, and put the phone back in her bag. She quickly washed and dusted her face with makeup. Surprisingly, it lightened her mood. "Well, maybe this won't be so bad. It's been weeks since I had any fun, and he is cute," she said to no one in particular.

"Don't you two look great, brilliant, in fact." Jiao noticed, for the first time, a touch of a Hong Kong accent in Kang's greeting. "This is my brother, Yi, and he works at another factory." Jiao also noticed, unlike Kang's clean hands, that Yi's were clean but the nails were dirty and his palms flashed with the ground-in dirt that she remembered from laborers. *What kind of work does he do?* she wondered.

The tearoom was in the heart of Dongguan, a city that still scared Jiao. To her, it was all chaos and noise. A few pigeons survived but they were like the people, strutting around in confusing circles trying to peck at each other. Cars filled the streets, bicycles filled the spaces left, but every day she heard about people being hit and killed. Even Jiao knew that thousands of cars, with inexperienced drivers, would always come out ahead in any collision. She had heard, during the last year, that three girls from the factory had been hit by cars while riding their bikes;

their spots at the sewing machines were quickly filled the next day. Jiao, Huan, and their dates took the bus.

The cakes were good, in fact, very good. The waitress kept bringing more, as well as small buns; the tea reminded her of home. It was turning into a nice evening. Kang told funny stories of his home about an hour north by train. His great-uncle ran a school there. He learned about the world and everything he needed to get ahead from this school and his uncle. His family members were good friends with the owners of the factory; their two families came from the same village. Jiao sensed a touch of pride; it didn't seem like bragging.

"That means you're rich, right?" Huan blurted. *Leave it to Huan to say the first thing that comes to her mind,* thought Jiao.

"We're doing okay," answered Yi. He had been very quiet for most of the evening. "Yes, we're comfortable."

Jiao watched Kang give Yi a strange look.

"Enough about us," Kang said. "Jiao, you're from the mountains where the earthquake hit?"

Jiao was jolted by the change in the conversation. "Yes, almost two years ago now; I'm getting over it slowly. I lost everyone, even Mei now, since she ran away."

"Yes, she was a pretty girl, too bad. Ever hear from her?" Kang asked.

Jiao looked at Kang for a minute, her mind racing. *Should I?* she asked herself. "I still miss her. No . . . I haven't. It's like she disappeared from China."

Kang studied her for a moment, then changed the subject again.

"Let's get a bite to eat. There's a great little sushi place around the corner—it's very cool. I'll make sure you get home to wash your hair, Jiao, no worries."

"Oh, Jiao washed her hair last night. Took almost an hour in the bathroom, made the girls furious. Isn't that right, Jiao? Last night, right?" Jiao knew she could count on Huan to keep a secret, the idiot.

Kang smiled, but didn't say anything.

With Huan's comment, there wasn't a way that Jiao could refuse dinner, and sushi was a treat, so exotic, so foreign. They walked the two blocks; a small table in the rear was available, almost like it had been held for them. Jiao knew this was impossible; she was sure even Kang didn't know where they would end up. The booth had a curtain that separated it from the rest of the room, nicely decorated, and the cushions were comfortable. Within seconds after they sat, the first course of prawns and rice arrived, along with a large warm pot.

"Have either of you ever had sake? It's a delicious drink made from rice. Helps to clean the tongue after these spicy foods. Huan, you go first."

"Goody, I've never tried it, but I've heard of it, very foreign and mature." Huan took a sip from the small cup, and coughed. "Kind of catches you, doesn't it?" She laughed and took another sip.

"Be careful, Huan," Jiao said. "Pretty strong stuff."

"Now you, Jiao, now you."

Jiao waved her hand. "Maybe later."

"Come on, Jiao, this is the mild stuff, real easy on the throat." Yi stuffed a piece of rice covered with a green sauce in his mouth. "Come on, give it a try."

Jiao picked up the small porcelain cup and held it out for Kang. "That's my girl."

She took a sip of the warm liqueur. *Not too bad,* she thought, *not too bad.*

They drank two more pots of sake and ate plates of sushi, so many that Jiao lost count. Huan insisted that they go to the restroom together; when they returned, the boys had great big smiles on their faces. Jiao thought to herself, *Well, now here it comes. I remember a little of what my aunt told me about dealing with forceful boys. Let me see if I can remember.*

The boys insisted on another drink, a toast, in fact, to their dates. To Jiao, it tasted the same but a little different. She knew her tongue was a bit numb from all the sake, but this was different, bitter.

"This is real tasty," Huan said. "You saved the best for last."

The two boys looked at each other and smiled. Jiao didn't like their looks, and she thought of the big cat at home when it had a mouse trapped under its huge paw. Yes, that was what she remembered as the room began to spin; she watched Huan's large eyes look to the ceiling before she fell over backward onto the cushioned lounge. When Huan landed on the couch, Jiao turned to Kang. "You son of a bitch," was all she could spit before she passed out.

To Jiao, the world was a cold dark place; at least her headache was gone, but there lingered darkness worse than the blackness all around her. Only a small, very dim overhead light illuminated the room—she could only make out the faint outline of her hand. She heard snoring, and then a profound sense of disorientation, as her world seemed to slowly shift to her right; then, after a pause, slowly return to normal, then to the left, like she was rocking back and forth.

11d

Basil snuggled his muzzle against Sharon's thigh, and she scratched the top of his head. "It's a bitch, my boy. Mom has to work a little harder; seems we are running out of money before we run out of the month." Bills and papers covered her desk. Her Beretta, now returned from the crime lab after testing, held down one of the larger stacks.

"You okay?"

Sharon turned to Evelyn Luca, standing at the door to the small office; she held a cup of coffee. "Want one? I just brewed it."

"Love one, thanks," Sharon said, as she watched Luca leave.

For two weeks, Luca had been O'Mara's roommate, two long and difficult weeks. Sharon never thought of herself as an overly private person, but now, with a stranger in the house, she found that she preferred just the company of Basil and an occasional guest. She never had privacy in the Army, but now she found that she liked living alone; her house was a blanket that she wrapped around herself. Now there was someone under the blanket and she was getting uncomfortable. Luca was never a bother; neat, in fact overly neat, she even cleaned the house, to Sharon's embarrassment. She cooked like that Italian broad on the Food Channel and, to her surprise, she hadn't gained the expected pounds. It was the simple fact that Evelyn Luca was always there, on the couch, in the kitchen, sitting on the patio in the sun, or in the bathroom. It was there that wars might be fought. The tight counter space was adequate for Sharon O'Mara, but not for the daughter of one of Italy's most famous fashion houses. Luca had a small suitcase of vials, tubes, brushes, and jars, and at any time there might be ten items lying about. It was here that she felt the most crowded. Standing in front of the mirror one morning, all she could say to herself was, "This has got to be over soon, real soon."

Luca insisted that Sharon use the retainer as part payment for the rent; Luca would buy the food. Sharon reluctantly agreed; she held a secret fear this arrangement could be permanent.

Luca returned with the coffee.

"Being self-employed isn't all it's cracked up to be, Evelyn. I get to run my own schedule, do what I want, and be broke most of the time. Thanks for the help and for the job."

"You're welcome, and thanks for the room; the time has let me sort some things out. I talked to that guy from Homeland and he said everything is okay. I get my computers and my shop back on Monday; you know most of the rest. Nothing more on Lau; he thinks she may have disappeared. So I need to leave you and Basil and get back to my place." Luca must have seen the change of expression on Sharon's face.

"I know, I live alone, too, remember? I would hate it if I had to put someone up, even if it was my idea. It's been great but I'll have to leave, probably tomorrow. Italy is all up in arms over the plans and drawings of the new designs; they're trying to find out who stole them. They're even considering changing the design a bit to foil these counterfeiters; it's an expensive option, but it might have to be done. I would hate to have our product trumped by fake bags months before we release them. The other design houses would just love to look into our bags to see what they could copy."

The photos that Jiao sent to Norma Chang surprised Luca. The plans were the same drawings they approved for the coming fall line of handbags. Luca told Sharon that there was only one place these plans could have been taken from, their design studio in Florence. All the design and creative work was under tight security—a cousin controlled the shop. Somehow these plans ended up in a leather factory in Dongguan. Luca contacted her brother, the company's president, and sent him copies of the photos. He was shocked; he told her he would find out what happened, and do it quietly. The company didn't want the publicity and Luca agreed.

"You have been great, and it's been your work that busted this up. My company is grateful; my father told me to offer you a bonus of ten thousand dollars. I hope it helps a bit."

Shocked, Sharon agreed. *Maybe I can get this gig to work. Wouldn't Travis McGee be pleased,* she thought.

"Thanks, Evelyn, yes, it helps a lot. Thanks."

Luca left and Sharon turned back to the stack of papers on her desk, licked the last of the envelopes, and stuck stamps to their corners. "Maybe this electronic bill-paying thing will save a few dollars a month; certainly save some postage. Should get around to doing it. At least with the car gone, I don't have insurance and gas bills, but it sure cramps our style getting out, doesn't it, Basil?" His head rose at hearing his name. "Yeah, you're the one that doesn't get to the park as often as you want, and I'm sure Kevin is getting a little tired of hauling us around. At least I'm eating well between Luca and the kindness of strangers."

Sharon had dinner with Inspector Detective Lopez the night before at Boulevards, along the Embarcadero in San Francisco. Kevin managed to talk Sharon into allowing him to tag along; in fact, when she mentioned it to Lopez, he immediately agreed. "I would like to meet this man that seems to have your heart, or thinks he does, yet does not have the courage to ask for it."

"Xavier, that's not what it's like at all. We are just good friends and there's too much baggage between us anyway," Sharon said, trying to turn the conversation.

"The only baggage we have is that which we carry ourselves. Besides, he sounds like an interesting man, so enough said. I have made reservations near the BART. Is that okay? I remember what you said and the concierge said it's an excellent restaurant, si?"

"Si, it's very, very excellent, Xavier."

And it was. Sharon's rabbit ravioli was sublime, Lopez's prime rib hung over the plate, and Kevin's pork chop, over an inch thick, could almost be cut with a fork. Sharon watched the two men eat their meat like the street soldiers they were. Juice trailed from the corner of their mouths, was quickly dabbed away, and then reappeared with the next bite. She smiled at the carnal appeal of the steaks and red wine laid across the table. The evening had turned into a feast of drinking and food. Between the salads and second plates, two people, a man and a woman, walked up to the table and Lopez introduced them as two sub-assistants to the assistant to the under-secretary of ports and shipping security for Homeland Defense. They were involved with the conference. To Sharon's eye, they were a lot more than assistants to each other; their body language said: dinner's over, we saw people, did our duty, now time for dessert—who was whose dessert still remained to be negotiated. She quickly calculated how much this little dinner and the sub-assistants to the assistant to the under-secretary cost, times how many others at the meeting and our government's need to have these international conferences. It would be cheaper to send the money to the drug lords and buy them off. *Stop that, Sharon O'Mara, your cynicism is showing,* was all she could offer as a defense.

"So you're the famous detective Kevin Bryan; Sharon has talked a lot about you." Surprisingly, it didn't sound condescending to Sharon; Lopez actually said it with respect.

"I guess I am," Kevin said, with a touch of Irish humility. "Sharon shouldn't say so much about me; I'm just a cop in a small town." He looked toward Sharon.

"We are all cops from some small town; unfortunately, it's the big towns that need our help, too. Take this conference, and, by the way, tell your government thank you for the wonderful hospitality. Everyone attending has run into some trouble with these gangs from Mexico and China, and the problem is now growing with competition from Eastern Europe and even Israel. Sharon, where there's money and vice, there will be merchants, merchants of death. They move about with such ease; it's a wonder we can even stay ahead of them."

"I thought Baja's problems were less than the rest of Mexico," Kevin said.

"Un poco, but we still have all the same desires, Señor Bryan. And when tens of thousands of tourists from around the world come to visit our clean air and delightful beaches, they also seem to want many of the recreational drugs and other things that come with them. The cartels are more than happy to supply them. I'm very concerned about what it's doing to our children. Years ago, the children, even as poor as they were, could face a reasonably good life; now there's too much competition for their souls. That is where my efforts lie, to try and change how these gangs affect our youth, the boys and the girls. Like your young lady from China, the young girls from Baja Sur also leave home or are kidnapped to work in Mexico City and Monterey and God knows where else. That's what I'm trying to change. It's very, very hard."

Sharon thought of charter captain Gregorio's children and was saddened to think about where they might end up. "Gregorio is a good man, if he can only keep his boys focused on a good future."

Standing under the lights from the Bay Bridge, after dinner, Sharon and Lopez lit up their favorite tobaccos. Kevin was stunned by the size of the cigar that Lopez extracted from his suit coat pocket. "Kevin, this is a Te Amo Churchill, made in my country. They are trying very hard to make Mexican cigars as good as those from Nicaragua and Honduras, but it's difficult to teach the proper making of the cigar. But they try. I enjoy this one but there are many fine cigars to pick from, so I am, as they say, eclectic in my choices."

"They're both stupid and expensive habits." Kevin looked at Sharon.

"Don't start, Kevin," she replied.

"All I know is what I know."

"Well, you don't know everything."

"Stop it; you two sound like a couple of bickering teenagers. Smoking has its positives and negatives, I certainly agree. But for me, it's a touch of the rush and my personal drug of choice. You see, we all choose our vices; some just get more out of hand and become dangerous. A fine cigar isn't a threat to anyone, until you make it illegal, then watch what happens." Lopez watched the rich cloud of smoke rise toward the Bay Bridge and soften the thousands of lights hung in arcs between the towers.

Chapter 12

"**Dongguan** says the girl may be alive," Doris Lau said to Hong Feng. "They know her cousin at the factory; she came with the girl from the mountains. Even though she denies having a phone, one of our people is certain she's talked with Deng Mei."

"Good, then that will go away. I will make certain myself."

"It's already been done; she's in one of the six containers coming over here and she will arrive in two weeks. This time they won't go through Mexico; they'll go north through Vancouver, then come here. Vancouver is getting two of the boxes—what's in them, I don't know or care. What the Canadians need, I don't have a fucking clue, but our boxes have almost everything we need and they will have replacements for some of the girls; they're in the container with the girl's cousin."

"Good, I'll take care of her when she arrives. The usual transfer numbers and RFIDs, I assume?"

"Yes, at sea the containers will have new numbers and tags, and then they'll disappear at the port like normal. There'll also be a new manifest with the new numbers and, this time, don't lose the damn boxes. I don't want the same problem that we had last time after the transfer to San Francisco when those two idiots and that O'Mara bitch blew it up. Take them to the south Oakland warehouse." Lau waved her hand like she was dismissing nobody. Since the shooting of the girls, Feng had been very aware of her displeasure and her attitude.

This must change soon, he thought to himself, *very soon.*

Guangdong Province's most important tattoo artist inked the tattoo on Hong Feng's forearm. He tattooed exclusively for the family, and the red tattoo on Feng's arm had softened over the years and lost its sharp edge. Feng's own ancestral roots were interwoven into the family's history for hundreds of years. They had been foot soldiers and muscle and were proud of their strength; his brothers were now spread across the world. His father, still alive after many assassination attempts, still lived in a small village an hour from Guangzhou by train. He lived with six bodyguards and trained future soldiers for the family. The fools at the apartment complex were not a product of his father's training; they were street thugs from Hong Kong. This would change. It was Lau's expediency that caused the trouble and more thought must go into the management of the family's business.

The warehouse was not new in the sense of crisp stainless steel and dark glass, but it was new because the paperwork had been woven through so many holding companies and owners with Anglo names that the trail was certainly lost. The chaos of the current round of bank foreclosures had nothing on the ability to hide a land deal when there was money passed between brokers and title companies. The property even fell off the assessor's grid, lost in a series of fake parcel mergers and minor parcel maps. The property contained over twenty thousand square feet, two floors, no windows in the walls, bulletproof skylights, and two secured rooms for guests from China as they passed through Oakland on their way to being forgotten.

Feng made every effort to reduce the effects of the comings and goings to this building. A faded painting on the concrete block wall over the roll-up doors said "Bright Laundry"; no Chinese characters were visible on any wall or door. They used three step-vans as the only access in and out of the building. Each was painted with a faded graphic of a starched shirt and "Bright Laundry" text. No phone number or address was visible and no one ever tried to call. Feng thought the idea of a Chinese laundry cover was demeaning.

The interior was the opposite of the exterior. Racks held secured steel boxes and cabinets. Six steel shipping containers lined one wall, padlocks secured their doors. The upper floor was a mezzanine; a narrow catwalk accessed rows of offices and smaller rooms. Weapons fired from the walkway could cover every area of the floor. At the rear of the building, a stair accessed a long shooting range that ran under the concrete floor of the building. Here, under the ground floor, was a hidden passageway used to enter and leave the building. Buyers would be brought to the building in one of the vans, allowed to see and use the weapons, and then were required to leave. The guns would be delivered at the time and location chosen by Feng, after the money was deposited in a secured account. Even Feng arrived and left in one of the vans; his guards were all cousins more loyal to him than to the family. Lau had no control over his men; Feng knew that if he told them to kill her, her body would disappear so completely that it would be as if she had never existed. He also knew, because of her bungling, the family would have no alternative but to proceed with her replacement at some point. The only reason she remained alive was because she was profitable, very profitable; Feng bided his time.

The warehouse, where the girls had been kept, was now a garage; he kept his Mercedes there, as well as other family cars. A few of the new men, with false papers from China, now bunked in the garage until they learned some degree of English and lost some of the hardscrabble look of their China upbringing. For some, the look never left their eyes. Feng also made sure they didn't acquire too many of the tastes of Californians; these men were closely watched and trained. Feng's father did an excellent job teaching all the military and physical aspects of being a family soldier; it was one of Feng's jobs to make sure they blended in to California. Some, in time, would move on to Los Angeles, Seattle, and even New York, if they gained Hong Feng's trust and approval. It's what these men lived for.

12b

Basil still hobbled with a bit of a limp in his get-along; Sharon did all she could to help her best friend and make him comfortable, but once in a while he would give her a look that would strum the strings of her heart. He was now able to do a bit of a jog with her in the morning, more of a fast walk; it helped shake the stiffness out of him. His appetite returned and the weight loss lessened. Sharon was sure that more of the food was staying in than leaving; he looked fuller.

"That's a good boy, you're looking better, and thanks again." She pushed her head into the scruff of his neck; her red hair dragged across his face. Basil was in heaven.

Evelyn had been gone less than a week and their schedule seemed to be getting back on track. She set a bowl of water and fresh food on the kitchen floor. Basil cocked his head; he knew what was coming—the mistress was leaving for a while. He dreaded these times, and, in his youth, he showed it by demolishing bits of furniture and good carpets. Now, older and more mature, he knew she would return. But he did miss the good old days when she would pay special raucous attention to him after she found bits of the house chewed into hundreds of pieces. Yes, she did appreciate him, even if her yelling was loud. Now, off to bed, she wouldn't be gone long.

Sharon walked to BART and took the train west to the Lafayette station. Gino's sat on Mt. Diablo, a short walk in the amber sunset. The western hills glowed, the fog stayed well offshore; the evening was pleasant.

"Where the hell have you been? Last time I saw you, you were in the hospital after that BART thing. I'm very disappointed that you haven't come to see me, Sharon O'Mara," Gina Cavelli said.

"I have absolutely no excuse, and I ask for your pardon. I come to ask for forgiveness due to my lack of manners and propriety. When people come to your deathbed, the least you can do is visit them, if you live. Gina, my dear, I supplicate myself before you within this holy shrine."

"That's better; now come and give me a hug."

Gina Cavelli ran the best drinking establishment in Lafayette, maybe in the whole county. She had washed the floor and polished the bar for at least forty years, but she wouldn't admit that to anyone. Her father had been the high priest of the establishment, for as long as any of the recent residents could remember; the bar was well worn when the Japanese attacked Pearl Harbor. Gina's great-grandfather, Geno Sr., came from Genoa to fish the rich waters off San Francisco. After the San Francisco earthquake, and a wall that fell on his leg that left him with a serious limp, he found an empty building in the small village of Lafayette. They moved from their burned-out house in San Francisco and lived upstairs over their new bar. His wife, Rosa, served spaghetti and lasagna that kept them open, through Prohibition, with the food from the kitchen and the red wine hidden in the cellar. The Cavellis had three sons. One died in Italy during the war; another became a banker; and Geno Jr., when he returned from the war, took over the bar. Gina was the third-generation Cavelli to run a liquor confessional in Lafayette; she was a solid member of the community and took no guff from anyone. A few years earlier, a thug walked into the bar and demanded that everyone put their valuables in a bag. More concerned with his own theatrics, he didn't notice the thirty-five-inch Willie Mays Louisville arc through the air and part his hair; he lived, and her reputation grew.

"The usual?"

"Please," Sharon answered, setting the orange handbag on the counter.

Within seconds, a double Johnny Walker sat in front of her. Gina looked at the bag. "Well, excuse me, Ms. Sharon O'Mara; I guess the detecting biz is working out for you real well. A STIA, only in my dreams; good God, girl, and in my favorite color."

Sharon smiled and stroked the bag. It did feel soft.

"Gina, let me tell you a story that does not have an ending, yet." Sharon took a sip; the cool liquor warmed her throat until it found a home. She told Cavelli the history of container shipping on the West Coast from her particular point of view. Another drink later and Gina stood stunned behind the bar.

"Shit, in your own home. The sons-a-bitches deserved everything they got, and it's good that Basil is doing okay. Guns, sex slaves, junk, and handbags, holy hell, but damn them to hell, too. Who the fuck do they think they are?" Gina said.

"That's what I'm trying to find out. This gig is paying okay, actually may even work out, but there're too many loose ends. Who's stealing the designs and where are the girls? The Feds can handle the guns; I'm more concerned with the girls. Something smells at the port—too much is getting through, and too easily. What?" Sharon looked at Gina and the smile on her face. A soft breeze tickled her ear and an Irish mug stared at her in the mirror behind the bar.

"If it isn't Detective Kevin Bryan. After all these months, I get a two-fer, the dynamic duo that saved Lafayette."

"Be careful, Kevin, she's in an unforgiving mood. She thinks we have been avoiding her, something about maybe seeing other bartenders on the side."

Kevin stretched his tall frame over the bar and gave Gina a long kiss.

"That's better, but you're still about five of those short," Gina said, expectantly.

Kevin obliged and then kissed Sharon on the cheek.

"Sharon, I certainly wouldn't accept that, what a piker. If the man was Italian, I would've dimmed the lights. Irish—good God, man, where's your soul?"

"Fine, whatever." Trying to make some amends to the ribbing, Kevin stood Sharon up from her stool, pushed away her red hair, and planted a full, warm kiss on her shocked lips. Three seconds passed, then four.

"Break, I said to kiss her, not cause a scene that might cost me my license," Cavelli said with a laugh.

Sharon was shocked. Kevin had kissed her hundreds of times, casual nips and cheek things, but this kiss was different. She wasn't sure if she liked it or feared it.

Kevin asked for a Jameson on the rocks and saddled up next to Sharon.

"Mei's very upset; she's tried to call Jiao for three days and there's no answer. The service is still on—at least that's what Norma says; only she can understand the chatter when she tried

China information. Just seems like the phone is off or out of power. I'm concerned as well. Norma's doing okay, but Sergeant Chang knows his mother is covering up her fear for Mei. These bastards will do anything; that, I'm sure of."

Sharon's phone started to play the Mexican Hat Dance.

"What the hell is that?" Then Kevin realized: "Lopez?"

"Si." She flipped the phone open. "Xavier, what's up?"

Sharon listened and motioned to Gina for a pen; she started to write on a napkin: six containers . . . left China . . . PCL . . . due next week.

"Thanks, Xavier, yes . . . yes, I will tell him, yes, thank you, I did have a good time . . . I'll let him know. Lunch, maybe later. You, too, soon . . . Buenos noches."

"His contacts in China say that six containers have left Chiwan, the same port that our first four left from, including the one with the bodies in Cabo. They tracked the shippers back through the manifests. They only found out after the ship left port. Two of the boxes are headed for Vancouver and four are listed for Oakland. The manifest says that the boxes have farm equipment in them."

"At least they could be more original, don't you think?" Gina said with a wry smile.

12c

Jiao's first thought was that she was in a tomb, but tombs don't rock; they never rock back and forth. Only ships rock back and forth, not tombs. A light clicked on at the rear of the room and suddenly cots appeared; a dark shape wrapped in a blanket bent over the small lamp. Boxes lined the walls, large bottles were mounted in crates, plastic coolers were secured with cords, under every cot were more boxes marked with their contents, most contained food. Large signs hung on the walls, all covered with Chinese characters. The largest said: "Do not make a sound or you will be removed and killed."

The small light at the top of the container changed from light to dark four times; she thought it must be an air vent or a gap in the steel plates. Jiao remembered that Mei had said she thought it changed twenty times before the boat stopped rocking, then she lost count. There were ten other girls in the container; Huan stopped crying on the second day. The seasickness had turned the box into a mess that they were finally cleaning up; no one had been sick for three days. The food was good, considering where and how they were trapped. One girl laughed and said that it was better than the jail that she spent a month in when she was arrested in her hometown before she went to work at the factory. "I have more room and a bed for myself," she added. Jiao thought she was crazy.

Jiao believed the sign and information on the walls. Why shouldn't she? Maybe they would kill them if they were found, just thrown overboard, never to be found. Two of the girls organized the food and took inventory—three battery lamps lit the steel room; extra batteries were in a box. All the food was cold, but at least the water was clear. Jiao would love to have a cup of tea, but there would be none of that. One of the organizers said that they had enough food for twenty-five days; she suggested they ration the food in case the trip took longer. Huan objected.

"If I'm gonna die, I'm gonna die with a full stomach." The others thought the idea of rationing was a good one; they watched Huan to make sure she didn't take more than her fair share. Jiao was sure that she was stealing biscuits when they were asleep.

Jiao had her warm coat—it was the only thing she could thank Kang for; he knew what was coming and he knew the coat would help keep her warm. Her cell phone was buried deep in a pocket. She was glad that she hadn't left it in her bag, which was now gone. The box's walls were like the interior of a refrigerator. She understood that she was lucky; someday, if she lived, she would kill Kang, that son of a bitch. For someone who was three months past seventeen, she had certainly grown up since the earthquake. Two of the girls wrapped themselves with their blankets; never taking them off, hygiene was the first casualty. The pots used for the toilet needed to be changed; one girl suggested putting the waste back into the empty water bottles, and they each took turns with the foul job. Even Huan agreed and joked that, as a child, she did this at her grandfather's farm; she would carry it to the night soil box that would become fertilizer after it aged. They played card games, and mahjong; they found two boxes of the tiles under some boxes of biscuits. Jiao dreamed of shoving one tile after another down Kang's throat with a stick.

On day fourteen, there was banging and clanking noises on the side of the box; they could only imagine what was going on. They kept quiet; none wanted to risk being thrown into the sea.

"Jiao, do you think we are going to America?" Huan asked. "I have heard they use Chinese girls as slaves in America. We must do what we are told or they will kill us."

"I don't know, Huan. I don't think so," Jiao said. "They must be very rich to afford the handbags and leather goods that we make. I know we could never buy them. So why would they have slaves and such? They could pay to have anything they wanted. We'll see, I'm sure, just be quiet and go back to sleep. Even this will be over soon."

They realized that they were in a port when noises banged all around them. Then the rocking would begin again. For three days, the seas rolled heavily front to back and side to side. Seasick again, they were beyond caring about the smells and vomit across the floor. At least they could still drink water, but they were down to their last two bottles. Jiao hoped the trip would soon be over or she would welcome the relief of death.

Chapter 13

13a

"**Sharon**, we found out who stole the plans," Evelyn Luca said, looking over the rim of her cocktail. "He was my nephew, my brother's son. Ever since he returned from college, he's been full of these notions of society and righteousness. He confessed that he did it . . ."

". . . for strange reasons only he can understand," Sharon said, interrupting.

"Yes, bottom line was he needed money, a lot of money. His father has always been frugal and requires that his children diligently manage their money. Paul didn't and burned through a lot of cash in college and developed a taste for gambling. Eventually, he lost too much in a Macao casino and the people he owed gave him an out. He has been giving them plans for the last three years; no wonder they were so quick to show up on the streets."

"Money will do that, debt even more."

"After his father explained the effects of what he did, with the deaths in Mexico, the girls, and the shootings, I think he began to realize that his actions had consequences, some dire and some life-threatening consequences. He will be watched closely, for both family and business reasons. He also developed a drug problem in Macao—from the same people. So it's going to get rough before it gets better for him."

Sharon signaled the bartender with two fingers; he quickly responded. She took a sip of her Johnny Walker Blue. *Too smooth,* she thought, *but at least I'm not buying.*

"Where is he now?" she asked.

"In a clinic in Switzerland, addiction therapy and a bit of what we call family house arrest."

"How nice for him; better than some shit hole in Macao or

China."

"One way to put it, and yes, it's better than anything an Italian court would do. He's lucky; maybe he'll get it out of his system before someone else is hurt."

"They were doing these things long before Paul was even born. This is a huge operation and we are looking at only one small part. My guess is that your bags are just a small piece of a forgery and knockoff syndicate; they're probably doing much worse elsewhere."

"Probably. Anyway, we have changed the designs, just a bit, but enough to throw them off. Two new colors and we're starting to emboss a pattern into the leather, a difficult and meticulous process, one that makes it too expensive for a knockoff operation but not a problem for our line. When you see it, I think you will like it, a lot."

"Yes, I know. Me, I like Jaguars—the cars, not the cute furry things. But what I like and what I can afford are two very different things."

Lunch was a crab sandwich at Tadich Grill; Luca had a plate of oysters. Sharon still couldn't get herself to eat them raw; wrapped in bacon and grilled, she would eat a dozen, but slide them down her throat all slippery and such—much too much.

It was Luca's idea for lunch as a way of settling all the outstanding bits of her contract and to finish things. Sharon wasn't sure if Luca got her money's worth, considering the Feds and the police issues, but they were in the past now. Luca was back in business and it looked like the knockoff issue, at least for now, was also over. There was money in the bank, Basil had food, and she had started thinking about buying a car.

"How is that young Chinese woman, Sharon? Is she doing okay?"

"Deng Mei is doing very well. She was lucky, very lucky. Turned into the right teashop at the right time; yes, timing is everything."

"Good, and your Detective Lopez—he is okay?"

"Evelyn, let's not go there, please. Detective Lopez is a gentleman with a high opinion of himself, probably justified now that I know him better. But life is complicated enough to include a long-distance relationship. Cabo San Lucas is my escape. If he's there then there's nowhere to go to get away. I need Cabo— my Cabo."

"Mine is Capri," Luca said. "I have a small cottage that hangs on the side of a cliff. It catches the morning sun and is cool in the afternoon heat; a small terrace allows me to sit and ignore the world. There's only one bedroom and not another bed, anywhere. When the evenings are warm and delightful, I pull the bed out onto the terrace and sleep under the stars; the surf rolls up the cliff and echoes through the olives. I miss it. Now, not sure when I will see it again; won't be for a while."

"Same for Cabo. To our private lives and secret lovers." Sharon raised her glass, Luca as well.

"To secret lovers."

After lunch, Sharon walked to the Embarcadero waterfront. It bustled with joggers and tourists. Tank tops and suits strolled the concrete, each lost in their own thoughts and iPods. A long pedestrian pier stuck out into the Bay, the sides lined with benches. She stopped and lit a cigarette near the end of the pier. The tide was low; a ferry carved its double hull through the water, at almost twenty knots, as it pushed its way toward the cultural island of Marin County.

Her phone buzzed in her butt pocket; she had not turned on the ringer since she left the restaurant.

"Hi, Kevin . . . San Francisco . . . lunch with Evelyn Luca . . . No, I'll be heading back shortly. The boat left Vancouver this morning, due in the day after tomorrow, in the morning, good. How about dinner with you and Lopez tomorrow? . . . Come on, Kevin, get over it. He's leaving the day after the ship arrives, quit acting so stupid; he's fine and a complete gentleman . . . believe what you will. I'll set it up, see if he's available. If not, just you and me then."

Her call to Lopez was short; he was on a break between lectures. His eagerness to see her, regardless of Kevin's company,

lightened her afternoon. The ride home on BART was easy—
rush hour was still an hour away.

13b

Feng returned to the warehouse; he knew Lau would still
be in a foul mood and would be until they unloaded the ship.
His man in Vancouver said the unloading there went without
a hitch. The two hundred pounds of heroin, and other pharma-
ceuticals, were quickly moved to a small warehouse north of the
docks. The other materials that filled the boxes were fireworks
and fake hockey memorabilia. Why someone wanted Canuck
sweatshirts, he still didn't understand, but they cost pennies to
make and sold for forty dollars apiece, very profitable and they
undercut the official sweats by ten Canadian dollars. The empty
container was transferred to their production warehouse where
it would be filled with British Columbian wine with fake Napa
Labels applied for the return trip to China.

"Where the hell have you been?" Lau demanded.

"Talking to Lin in Vancouver; everything is good there. The
boat is on its way here, day after tomorrow, early," Feng answered.

"Good, get the numbers and I will have the trailers ready."

"I have done this a hundred times, Lau, so don't worry. Even
after all the screw-ups, no one will be able to tell which box has
our goods inside. They can have an army waiting and, unless
they cut open every box, there's no way they can find them. The
captain will have ours removed and logged in separately and
Spinos will ensure that they're not bothered."

"I have not trusted that man since the beginning. He's not
family and, even though Europe vouches for his credentials and
experience, I don't trust him. Keep him at arm's length and tell
him only what he must know, nothing more."

"Always have and he's been good keeping the security tight
around our containers."

"Yes, like that fuckup with the last box with the girls. He lost
the fucking thing and had to use the Guard to find it."

"We couldn't just have our men walk around peeking into boxes, could we?"

"Would have been better."

"He made sure we heard about the container before the port police and we were able to slide in with our own people to get the girls before word got out. He was very helpful; I don't expect anything less. Besides, his small problem with smack doesn't hurt us either. With free drugs, money, and an occasional evening with one of the girls, you would think he was a rock star instead of a whiney Greek suburbanite. He'll not be a problem."

"Better not be and I still don't trust him."

"You don't trust anyone."

"Yes, remember that!"

Feng secured the last of the trailers that they would use to haul the boxes from the port; there was enough room in the warehouse to put the four in a two-abreast placement. The forklift would lift the boxes from the trailers and set them against the wall. Then the trucks could quickly exit and get back to the port, where they were normally stored. As far as the owner of the trailers was concerned, they had been used to run shipping containers to an almond ranch in the Central Valley. Again, Feng made sure the paperwork was thorough and completely false.

Feng realized that the Mexicans would not go away; they had been a pain in the ass for the past four years and were getting worse. The loss of his men and the girls at the apartment was only the latest show of their strength. He had two men who he thought might have passed on the information. He knew both were cocaine addicts, even though they did a good job of covering it up. The enterprises of the Oakland and San Francisco Chinatowns and Mexican cartels grated against each other. The Mexicans, with their Escalades, and the Chinese, with their Mercedes, raced around their respective urban territories like soccer moms and businessmen taking their kids to school in the suburbs; tinted windows hid their foreign faces from prying eyes.

The next day, Feng mapped out the routes and the process to the drivers.

"The containers will be set here and here," Feng said, pointing to a map of the PCL port terminal. "You will pull your rigs here and the gantries will load you after you hand them the paperwork."

"What if we're stopped?" one of the drivers said; he was also one of Feng's suspects.

"I will be in the lead truck and the boss will be in the second truck, you two will follow. Don't get lost or do something stupid; if you do, ask him what will happen." Feng pointed to the man with the bandaged hand. "How'd that fuckup work out for you?"

Li Yunxu slowly slid his hand from sight.

"After the containers are on the road, we will head straight here. They will be quickly pulled from the trailers and then you're out of here. It should take no more than an hour. Drop the trailer back at the yard near the port, then get back here. Remember, if you're caught, you're just drivers and the paperwork states that the boxes are going to another address. Deny everything—that's why you have been delivering containers all over Northern California for the last six months; deny it and get out. I'll help you when I can, but the best advice I have for you is, don't get caught or do something stupid."

* * *

Li Yunxu looked at Feng and nodded; he needed a quick snort. Li had slipped quietly into the United States five years earlier from a container ship docked in Long Beach, not as a passenger locked in one of the boxes, but as a deckhand who mysteriously disappeared from the ship's complement. The captain was pissed but he only reported it to his superiors in China; they, of course, never reported it to anyone else. His spot was quickly filled when the ship arrived back in Hong Kong. Yunxu's cousin picked him up at the terminal gate with false papers that included a driver's license and social security card. For the next year, he worked as a busboy and dishwasher in a small restaurant in Chinatown and did odd jobs for a man who owned a tourist gift shop. In time, he began to get full-time work driving containers full of Chinese trinkets from Long Beach to the man's three shops. With the extra money, he also developed a habit of sniffing cocaine; he hated alcohol, but cocaine was everywhere and easy to get, especially from some of the Mexican drivers. Within two years, he was addicted, but managed to keep it under control, or so he told himself.

"Li Yunxu, I need a man to work with me in Oakland," Doris Lau said. "You have been very loyal to my father and I'm moving north to help with the family business. Do you want to work with me there?"

To be asked his thoughts was beyond anything Li Yunxu had ever dreamed of. All his life he had been told what to do; he had never been asked what he wanted. A singular honor, Yunxu thought. "Yes, Ms. Lau, I will go with you."

He celebrated that night by getting very high with some Mexican drivers. They were good to him, and when he was a bit short, they would help him out with a line or two of coke. He knew them both as Jose and Paco; Li never learned their last names. They said they had been in Los Angeles their whole lives and drove for a shipping company in San Bernardino. He woke up the next morning all bloody and with the body of a young woman under his legs; Jose and Paco helped him out of the room.

"I don't know what to do; I don't even know who she is or why she was with me," Li said.

"Don't worry, Li, we have some friends that can help us; they can make this disappear but you need to find ten thousand dollars for their expenses," Jose said.

"I don't have ten thousand dollars; I don't even have a hundred. I need to talk with Ms. Lau; she'll know what to do."

"Bad idea, Li; she doesn't need your troubles. Besides, she will probably make you disappear first."

"She wouldn't do that!"

"Li, you know she would; you know what their business is, so you know she would. So you need to keep this from her. Go and try to find the ten thousand; we will take care of this mess you made. We'll talk tomorrow."

Five tomorrows came and went. Li grew more and more anxious as each day passed. He finally borrowed three hundred and forty dollars from some friends. He knew it was not enough, but maybe Jose and Paco's friends would let him pay the rest over time. The confrontation came as he climbed down from his rig at the port; Paco slammed him against the truck's door and put a large blade against his throat.

"The money, Li, now."

"I only have a little over three hundred."

"Not enough. I need to pay the guys who helped clean up your little mess; they want their money today. If I give them only three hundred dollars, they will kill me, and then I won't have the satisfaction of killing you, so maybe I should just gut you here and then take off, comprende?"

Li shook his head, resigned to the inevitable.

"Hold it, Paco," Li heard Jose's voice over the guttural roaring of the trucks in the yard. The knife slid out of sight. "Maybe there's something else Li can do. My friends have questions about the containers coming in from China and are looking to send things from the US and Mexico to China. Maybe Li here can help us get some of that information."

"Let me cut his throat and then we can get out of here; he's a piece of shit and a murderer. Let me kill him now; he wouldn't help us anyway. You know how these Chinks stay together."

"Now, Paco, please. Yunxu understands that we just need information to help both of our companies grow; don't you, Yunxu?"

Li Yunxu, wide-eyed, looked at Jose like he was his savior. He nodded.

Four years later, Li Yunxu was still a driver for the family business in Oakland. Lau made sure he was taken care of; he made a few dollars and would occasionally help Jose with information about what containers were due in the port. Jose said this arrangement would last only one year, which was two years ago. To make sure Li understood, a picture of Li and the dead woman was taped to the steering wheel of his rig one morning. Li never asked when his services would be terminated again. He was resigned to his fate, a fate that was as thick as the fog he plowed through on the Bay Bridge some mornings.

* * *

"Li, you paying attention?" Feng said.

"Yes, sir, no problem. I understand. The ship is arriving to-morrow. I'm driving the last trailer. I'll pick up the final box here—" he pointed to the map—"then follow you out the gate. Then I return here. That's it, simple."

"Don't fuck it up or she'll take another one of your worth-less fingers, or worse, maybe your dick." The other drivers paid as close attention to the orders as Li Yunxu did. Yunxu knew Jose needed this information, and soon. He also knew that there would be an ounce waiting for him when he returned to his rig, then he could finally relax.

13c

Sharon set the table with her best-mismatched china and silverware. Never one for setting an elegant table, she certain-ly valued a comfortable and inviting one. Basil sat on his bed and watched her walk about the room pulling plates and glasses from shelves and cabinets. Jazz played over the speakers that she placed outside the door to her reclaimed office; Luca was fi-nally settled in her own home. The music was a direct feed from KKJZ in Long Beach; Duke Ellington's band filled the repainted hallway with a jazzy beat.

"Meat," was the immediate response she got when she asked Kevin and Xavier what they wanted for dinner. A five-pound standing rib roast was forty-five minutes from its presentation, along with baked potatoes and all the fixings. Dessert was an apple pie she bought at Whole Foods.

"This is about as American as it gets, fellow," she said to the war vet on his bed. "All I'm missing is corn-on-the-cob to make it complete, but you can't have everything, and besides, the stuff looked too early, need to wait another month." The shift from Ellington to Gillespie was seamless.

The last two days had been full of meetings and preparations. Homeland was running the show. Lopez said to Sharon on the phone that they were so concerned about proper procedures that they seemed to have forgotten how fucked up things can get in a hurry, especially when they don't go as planned. If there was one thing Lopez said, it was that the American federales loved to plan things. Sharon suggested seven o'clock for cocktails; Lopez's contribution was wine, and Kevin brought the ice. Sharon hoped the wine would be a good one; one that he would have to put on his expense account. She knew the next day would be difficult; the *McDonald* was due in the morning. An intricate plan had evolved that would catch the Chinese as they retrieved the boxes, a plan with so many variables that she was sure it might fail. The trap had been set—would the rats rush in? What she appreciated, from firsthand experience, was that thugs would do what they do; their men were expendable, so shoot first, don't ask questions, and get out as fast as possible.

Precisely at seven o'clock, her doorbell rang and Basil let loose with a bass woof that would have given second thoughts to any postman on the street. He made three more barks at the door before Sharon pushed him away with her hip.

"That's enough, it's company; into the kitchen, now." She dried her hands on the dishtowel and watched Basil saunter into the kitchen; she reached for and turned the door handle. Before it was opened less than an inch, the door was slammed hard inward, knocking her to the floor. Two large Chinese men pushed their way into the room, guns held high. One put the heel of his boot on her chest, and pointed a gun at her.

"What the hell do you know about the *McDonald* and where did you get the information, bitch? Where?" She recognized Fat Boy from the warehouse.

"Don't know what you're talking about."

"Tell me now or this fellow here will find your dog and

shoot him, and he is a better shot than me."

"Too late, he's found you!" Sharon turned to the kitchen door as Basil exploded through the opening and took the man down before he could bring his weapon up. The man began to scream; Basil's jaw wrapped around his gun hand. she heard the crack of bone.

"Tell him to stop or I'll shoot you, now."

Sharon turned back to Fat Boy as his hand flexed, getting ready to fire. She watched his eyes widen from shock and surprise. A small hole magically appeared on the left side of his temple, an inch above his eye. Then she saw the newly painted hall receive a sprayed coating of gore as the man crumpled like a cheap dictator's statue after the revolution. The screaming of the other man had stopped; Basil stood over the man, hand in maw, waiting for Sharon's signal. The man didn't move a muscle, frozen with fear.

Kevin pushed his way into the hallway, shoving the door hard against the dead Chinaman.

"Nice dinner guests. I thought it was just three tonight, not five."

Sharon stood and again wiped her hands, this time to remove a bit of bloody spray. "Thanks for coming to my rescue." She turned and saw Lopez come in from the kitchen.

"Señorita, you really must remember to lock your back door; you never know who might just push their way in."

"Basil, release." The hound did as he was told, but his eyes never left the man on the floor.

Lopez looked at the man. "You understand English?" The man nodded. "Good, roll over and put your hands behind you, now." The man was whimpering, but did as he was ordered. Lopez looked at Bryan, who pulled a set of handcuffs from behind his back and tossed them to the detective; five seconds later, the man was secured. The cuffed man never took his eyes off Basil either.

"That was the son of a bitch from the San Francisco warehouse, the one that bolted. These assholes never give up," Sharon said. "He won't bolt now, but look at my hallway."

The Walnut Creek police were not happy, having to vis-it O'Mara's cottage for the second time in less than six weeks. Kevin again acted as mediator and facilitator; the injured man was pulled into a waiting squad car. The deputy coroner arrived thirty minutes later.

"Well, if it isn't Detective Kevin Bryan, Lafayette's finest hero and this time in Walnut Creek."

"Yes, it's me, Dr. Miller, and the sooner you process the scene and have this trash removed, the sooner we can have din-ner; that man there was here to kill a friend and, as you can see, it didn't work out well for him."

Dr. Ralph Miller was the deputy coroner. His career path and reality were on separate tracks at the moment; he was try-ing to get them synchronized. He was dressing for a fund-raiser when the call came in; he was in as much of a hurry as Kevin to move the body elsewhere. The CSI techs pushed their way into the already crowded hall and the living room. Sharon looked out the window; neighbors, arms wrapped around themselves, were talking to each other.

"Shit, I'm never going to hear the end of this."

"What?" Kevin said looking back at Sharon.

"Nothing, but there's going to be talk on the street, again. Damn it." Sharon raced into the kitchen; ten seconds later, she returned. "Caught it in time. The roast may be a little more done than medium. But the potatoes are good."

Lopez and Bryan looked at each other and smiled. "Sharon, I left the wine on the picnic table out back, didn't want it injured. Please get it before these blues find it. Silver Oak does not travel well during gunfights, or at least that's what I've been told. They may want it as evidence," Lopez said, with a grin.

The removal of the body and the final work on the crime scene took another three hours. Stanley Chen saw Kevin and Sharon as he pushed the gurney up the walk.

"Is this going to be a monthly thing? I could just put you on my regular route."

"Good evening, Stanley, and no, this will be the last time we will see you, I guarantee it."

"Sure, anything you say, Detective, but you're becoming a regular." Chen knelt down at the body and turned the arm over. "Look familiar, Detective?"

All three looked at the forearm of the Chinaman. A red square enclosed a Chinese character.

"Xue," was all Chen said.

"What zoo?" Lopez asked.

"Blood," was the answer he got from three people, at the same time

Chapter 14

The PCL *McDonald Dynasty* slid quietly under the Golden Gate Bridge in the early morning, after making its way down the West Coast from Vancouver. The fog still hung above the deck of the bridge, and the sunlight cut shafts of light between the hills above Berkeley, illuminating the bridge's top towers. The captain watched his man respond to the orders of the pilot; this was not the place to hit a bridge or anything. His ship's 935 feet were tough enough to control in the wide-open ocean; here in this confined space between San Francisco's waterfront and Alcatraz, with its currents and private boats, vigilance was critical. The thousands of containers stretched to the bow, and much of San Francisco Bay lay spread out ahead of him. The Port of Oakland's gantry towers stood silhouetted, as he made the turn under the Bay Bridge. The PCL terminal sat between the APL and Stevedoring terminals in the Oakland Estuary. The captain noted the lack of wind; docking would be easier this morning.

The crossing had been as expected—a storm chased them into Vancouver, but the voyage south, with its following sea, was pleasant by his standards. He was to drop over a thousand containers of Chinese and Korean goods and load twelve hundred boxes; most were packed with waste paper for pulping. He was getting tired of being America's garbage collector, but his salary and his home in Hong Kong made up for the blemish of his cargo.

At this port he would not leave the ship and, in fact, except for the purser who watched as they took on fresh fruit, meat, and vegetables for the crew, no one was to leave the boat. The captain didn't know how many people would be leaving his ship inside these containers, and, if he did, he probably didn't care. The family paid him to command the boat. What was in the thousands of boxes locked into the rails of his ship was not his concern. His charge was to make the turnaround and be out of the port in ten hours. There was a lot to do before he could leave. Hong Feng wanted to talk; he needed to hand over the papers for the new numbers on the boxes and he needed his money.

Within minutes after the ship pulled tight its hawsers against the port's wharf, and even before the ramp from the boat was set to the dock, three huge three-hundred-foot-high gantry cranes extended their arms over the stacks of shipping containers that stood eight boxes high above the deck of the *McDonald Dynasty* and more than ten deep into the ship's bowels. Below each arm hung a spreader assembly suspended on cables. This unique device, under the control of the operator, glided into the ship and grabbed and locked onto the four corners of a shipping container and pulled it up from the hold, cleared the adjacent stacks, and centered it over a waiting truck and trailer rig that straddled the railroad tracks that allowed the crane to slide along the dock. After setting the box on the trailer, the spreader would again be driven into the hold of the ship to grab and remove the next box. Another trailer pulled into the exact same spot as the first, waiting to receive its load. Another crane did the opposite and loaded the ship from trailers with outbound cargo. This dance would continue for the next nine hours.

The loaded tractor trailer would then be directed, by radio, to a spot in the yard where another gantry, this one on rubber wheels, would pull the box from the trailer and stack it with thousands of others. The multi-colored stacks stood six and seven units tall and in rows filled with hundreds of the boxes. This was not a safe place to be on foot, let alone on a tractor trailer rig.

14b

Deng Jiao recognized that this stop was different. For almost eighteen days, the girls had been locked in a world that progressively became hell. There was only one carboy of water left and two boxes of biscuits—everything else was gone. The other bottles contained the piss and crap of their imprisonment, and if they cared, their stench would have nauseated them. Two girls stayed on their cots and seldom moved. Jiao was sure that another, the tough one, was now crazy; she stayed in one corner, wrapped in her blanket, mumbling. The other seven bided their time in the dark—only one small lamp remained lit; the batteries for all the others were dead. Jiao understood how those lamps felt: used, powerless, and empty.

The boat hadn't rocked for hours; she could hear metal-on-metal ringing through the walls of their tomb. Above and then to one side, the metallic concussions banged like sledgehammers. Then the noises came from all around them. Jiao watched the girl across from her, as her eyes grew wide.

"What's happening, Jiao, will we be crushed?"

"I think the box is being moved," Jiao answered, as they felt a rise in the pit of their stomachs, not unlike what she felt when the elevator at her apartment building lifted them from the ground floor. Then the box swayed and suddenly dropped, and the girl squeaked like a trapped mouse. The box clanged again, metal on metal, then there was a forward motion, different than that of the past two weeks; the box bounced three times; they felt it turn and bounce twice again, then stop. More metal on metal, more motion, and then, with a deadened thud, the box stopped moving. The girls all held their breath, waiting to see what would come next, but nothing came, there was no change, their world did not move.

Jiao looked at the sign still taped to the wall: "Do not make a sound or you will be removed and killed." At this point, she didn't give a damn. Anything would be better than this.

Jiao slowly drew out the phone from her jacket. For the last two weeks, when she was sure the girls were asleep, she would briefly check the phone for time and date and a signal. The time remained the same as their stop two days ago; she was sure they were no longer going east into a different time zone. The phone's battery had degraded to less than a quarter of its power; the signal was strong, very strong. The other boxes no longer interfered with the signal. *Maybe I should try*, Jiao thought. *Maybe now is the time.*

She looked at the recently dialed numbers and found Norma Chang's number, and now, not caring that the other girls knew, she pushed the send button. One ring, two rings, three . . . then, "Hello, Jiao, where are you? We have been worried sick."

Jiao's heart exploded. "Mother Chang, I'm safe but we don't know where we are."

"We?"

"Yes, I'm with ten other girls, locked in a metal container like Mei was in. I have no idea where we are. I had to save my power and could not call. We need help real bad. Some of us are very sick." Jiao spit the words into the phone, afraid it would die before she could finish. "How can you find us, Mother, how?"

Norma passed the phone to an anxious Mei. "Talk to Mei; she needs to talk to you. I will go to another phone."

As the girls talked, Norma called Danny Chang and told him the situation. "They are probably on the ship that just arrived from China," Danny said, "the *McDonald Dynasty*. Lopez says that's the name of the boat his boxes were on. It's being unloaded now. Lopez is there with Nethermann of the National Guard and Homeland. The boat is scheduled to leave in six hours, and already five hundred boxes have been pulled, a lot to go through."

"Find her, Danny; this needs to be over."

"We will. I'll call you as soon as I know anything."

Mei turned and looked at Norma; fear once again held her face in its hands. "The phone went dead. How can we ever find her, Mother? Is she lost again?"

"We'll find her, Mei. We will find her."

Jiao stared at the phone, now dark. Even the time and date were gone; even the battery symbol. She knew it was dead. She looked at the girls; two were walking toward her unsteadily.

"You had a phone all this time and didn't try to call anyone.

Why?" the taller one demanded. "Why didn't you call for help?"

"I tried but the other metal containers blocked the signal. I could never make a call; it would just waste power. But I just called Deng Mei; she's in America, in Oakland. She says that they're looking for us."

"Mei ran away with a boyfriend," one girl answered sharply.

"No, she was kidnapped just like us, and taken to America. That's where we are, I think. Oakland, California," Jiao said.

"California? You've got to be kidding, and what's this Oakland? "

"A city in California, near San Francisco. Mei was rescued and is staying with a friend. I just talked with her; they're trying to find us, I tell you. Would you please listen?"

"That sign says it all to me; if we make any noise, they will kill us."

"Is it any better than this shit hole? Is this how you want to die, in your own crap and piss? Mei says they will find us and save us."

The girls looked at Jiao; the crazy girl in the corner howled and screamed. The others ignored her. "When will they find us?"

"I don't know, but soon. She says that her son is a policeman and they're searching for us near the ship. Soon, I hope."

This quieted the girls, except for the crazy girl who just rocked back and forth as if the box were still on the high seas.

14c

Nethermann and his squad dismounted from their Humvees.

"Should be near here; the port says the *McDonald* is unloading the boxes in this area, half-done, four hundred to go." Vaca watched the gantry pull another box from a trailer and set it on the ground, the bottom box for a new stack. At least another hundred stood in a military row behind it, seven high.

"Shit, Sergeant, if they're at the top, how the hell are we gonna deal with that?" Vaca said.

"Let's find the boxes and hope they aren't at the top, then. Okay, Corporal?"

"Sure, Sarge, sure."

Sergeant Nethermann split his squad into two teams, each with a tag reader to pull data from the RFIDs on the boxes. This would help him locate and identify the boxes he wanted. They also carried binoculars to read the numbers on the doors; some would be almost eighty feet away at the top of the stack. Nethermann had a list of the box numbers that Lopez had given him; these numbers came from his contacts in the port in China. There were four containers that he was interested in, four out of a thousand; the port gave them a location, but not which stack or where they were in the stack. This was work for boots on the ground.

Nethermann's radio squawked. "Sarge, found one, three up, next aisle over."

"Thanks, Dugan. Vaca, next row, get your team there, now."

The row was at least five hundred feet long, with a cross drive. The box they wanted was the third container up—the numbers and the tag matched one on their list. A forklift trailed their team; the union driver, an ex-Marine, smiled.

"That one." Dugan pointed. "Box matches the numbers; I'm not getting a feed on the RFID."

"That happens sometimes," the forklift operator answered. "But we have to believe the numbers; occasionally it's fucked up."

"Thanks, great, just great," Nethermann said.

The lift operator had secured a palette to the blades; Dugan climbed aboard and was lifted to the box's doors. He banged loudly. No reply.

"I guess no one's home; you want me to bust it open, Sarge?"

"Cut the lock and let's look," Nethermann said.

The doors were locked with a plate and hidden lock mechanism, making it impossible to cut the lock; a cutting torch was all that would work. Dugan stripped out the hose and lit the tip; in less than twenty seconds the plate was cut, and the lock snapped free. He whacked the lock with a small sledge; it broke free and bounced off the palette, landing on the asphalt. This wasn't the first lock the squad had cut; they'd all stood back.

"Throw the handles, right side first," Vaca said.

"Shut up, I know what the hell to do." Dugan pulled the handles and the door opened; the palette prevented it from opening fully. "Sarge, you gotta see this. I don't think this is one of them." The forklift backed up and the door swung wide open. A white Mercedes grill faced the soldiers. "Don't think we were looking for a car, were we?"

Nethermann looked at the grill. Korean plates hung below the three-pointed star.

"Son of a bitches switched the numbers; Dugan checked the numbers on the door."

"Damn, Sarge, good job, but if you look real close, you can see where they have repainted and touched up the original number. You think they put this number on one of our boxes?"

"I don't doubt it; now we have a real game of hide-and-seek. Get down and let's regroup. I'll call Homeland and get some input."

For the next five minutes, Nethermann talked with two Homeland agents and ATF—they were at the port headquarters. This was not enough of a threat to cause a full-fledged investigation. They just wanted the boxes.

"Roger," Nethermann said, and pointed to Dugan. "Take your team and work your way around the end of the pile. See if any boxes have brighter numbers or, in some way, look tampered with; if you see anything, call me."

"Yes, Sarge. My guess is same PCL type and style—easier to change the numbers if the damn things look alike."

"Good call. We'll work the rest of this row and meet you at the end." Two more gantry cranes stacked more containers at the end of the row. "Hurry or we'll never catch up."

Ten minutes staring at boxes and numbers finally turned up one suspect, stacked four up in a stack of five. Five of the numbers matched the numbers on the Mercedes container.

"That's a good sign—easier to change just a few than all of them," Nethermann said. "Dugan, we have a candidate. Get the forklift over here; this one's higher."

"Great," was all he heard over the radio.

A minute passed and the second team turned the corner; the forklift followed. Dugan rose to the container's doors. "Same locks as the last. Torch it?"

"Do it," Nethermann said.

When the cutting was done, Vaca reached for the handle and hesitated; a soft thud came from the container.

"You hear that?"

"I don't like this at all, Sarge," Dugan said. "My senses are in overdrive."

Nethermann had followed Dugan's little quirks and instincts before and he was more often right than wrong. "Weapons."

Vaca hoisted the M-249 SAW to his shoulder and so did a second squad member. The rest slipped the safeties off their M-4s.

"Do it, Dugan," Nethermann said.

Corporal Dugan swung the right side open and faced three men in street clothes holding AK-47s; they were as stunned as he was. He heard a sharp yell in Chinese; from over their shoulders, two dark canisters flew through the air.

"Grenade!" Dugan yelled.

Halfway through their arcs, the grenades exploded; bright lights and loud concussions filled the canyon of boxes.

"Flash-bangs," yelled Vaca, who had already closed his eyes when he saw the cans. Opening his eyes, he saw three ropes fly out the open door. The forklift operator had already punched the release and Dugan was sliding to the pavement, holding on for life. Vaca watched the door as two rifle barrels appeared and swung in an arc toward the squad. "No fucking way, assholes!" Vaca said, and let off two bursts into the container. The SAW left little to the imagination; the others opened up immediately after Vaca. The AK-47s stitched holes in the asphalt and peppered the containers on the opposite side of the alley. They were shooting blind. The left side door hid Nethermann's men. Two more grenades flew out the door.

"Shit," Nethermann yelled. "Grenades, real shit."

Five of the squad members dove into the gap between the stacks. Dugan and the ex-Marine took cover behind the forklift; Vaca and Nethermann hit the deck. The concussions were as loud as the flash-bangs, but a hundred times more lethal. Shrapnel cut into Vaca's thigh, while the Kevlar in Nethermann's helmet and vest saved his life; a small nick cut across the back of his hand. Dugan grabbed his M-4 from the floor of the forklift and swung it toward the doors; the left side exploded open. Three men jumped from the container and began to rappel down the boxes, firing as they fell. Four more, in the open doorway, sprayed cover fire over the men on the ground.

The forklift operator grabbed Vaca's SAW and fired at the men in the open door; all fell backwards into the box. The five Guardsmen leapt from their cover and opened up on the rappelers; two fell to the ground, hit multiple times. The last one swung around and took aim at Nethermann as he started to rise. Dugan pulled his service revolver and killed the man as he hit the ground. It was over in less than fifteen seconds; no other sound came from the box.

"Shit," was all Vaca could say, as the squad medic wrapped a broad tourniquet around his leg. "Shit, and goddamnit to fucking hell."

"We need to get up there and see what's left. You two take positions there across the alley; Dugan, you and Grimes take the lift to one side and get close; they will cover you. You okay?" Nethermann said to the Marine.

"Haven't had this much fun since the Gulf War; shit, those fuckers wanted to really kill us. Damn, Sergeant, goddamnit."

Nethermann posted his men; he also called in the battle to ATF. He could hear sirens blaring in the distance, but the metal canyons bounced the sound so he couldn't be sure where they were coming form, like that day with the girls in the box. Dugan took his position; the forklift slowly moved the two men toward the opening. Dugan threw his own flash-bang into the container and lit it up. No return fire. After one fast burst, he jumped into the box.

Nethermann waited; finally a hand signal, thumbs up. Dugan walked to the door.

"Good shooting, Marine; they're all down, two dead, four wounded, one badly. The place stinks to high heaven, like the other one, Sarge. I don't think they were expecting us; I think someone else was supposed to meet them, not citizen Army."

"You think, Dugan, you think?" was all Sergeant Nick Nethermann could answer.

Another Humvee turned the corner of the alley, and four men dressed in black jumped from the rear, *ATF* stenciled on their backs. Detective Inspector Xavier Immanuel Lopez climbed out of the passenger seat, swung up his own M-4, and walked up to Sergeant Nethermann.

"You okay, Nethermann? That cut looks deep," Lopez said.

"I'm okay; it's those sons-a-bitches that didn't know what hit them, and I think they were expecting someone else. They were ready to leave when we cut the door open. Only not the way they thought."

"Sarge, phone here," Dugan yelled from high above them. "It's been used within the hour, a local number. I'll bring it down."

Dugan handed the phone to Nethermann; there were only two recent calls, both to the same number, and both since the boat docked.

"Someone knows these guys are here and, after all this noise and shit, so do a lot of the port people. My guess is that our secret's out—must have had twenty trucks and gantries drive by as we were searching. For all we know, the other boxes may have already been loaded and are either on their way out or have left. This is not a bunch of amateurs," Nethermann said.

"Si, si, I agree," Lopez said, as he pulled his radio from his hip pocket. "Base, Lopez. Close the gate. We have hostiles down here. Send ambulances now; also send the coroner. It's one big fucking mess. We are missing three containers; the numbers have been switched and the RFIDs are down. We will need to check every box as it leaves."

"Thanks, Lopez, I didn't expect to see you here."

"Joint operation and I was in the neighborhood, as they say. Besides, it was my guys in China that called the containers in. You need anything?"

"Get the EMTs here as fast as possible; Vaca is hurting bad."

As if on cue, two red and white ambulances turned the corner of the stacks and headed toward Nethermann and his squad. Still wary, Nethermann clicked the safety off his weapon and waited casually. When a good-looking blonde jumped from the passenger side, he relaxed; he just loved a woman in uniform.

"I'm taking the Humvee to the gate to meet O'Mara and Bryan." Lopez's phone rang to the tune of San Francisco. Nethermann's smiled.

"O'Mara?" Nethermann asked.

"Si, good morning, Sharon . . . si, yes, Nethermann's men busted them up . . . Where are you? . . . I'll meet you there; I'm in a black Humvee that I've borrowed from your excellent ATF people . . . si . . . I'll call you."

Lopez walked up to the dead and wounded men still sprawled on the ground. More Humvees and ambulances turned into the street enclosed by the containers. All the downed men were Chinese and fit; they were prepared for the hardships of the trip, but were dressed to blend in, to disappear as soon as they were collected. These men were tough—their hands were hard, and their weapons were well used. They looked like the soldiers he arrested that worked for the cartels, only from Asia, not Latin America. To Lopez, all criminals began to look alike. He bent down and pushed up the sleeve of one man; the tattoo slowly emerged.

"Blood," was all he said.

Chapter 15

Sharon knew that it was Doris Lau; even the tint of the SUV's glass couldn't obscure the fact. The sharp shock of pink hair, the silhouette, the glare, it was all there. She flashed back on the late spring morning when Lau stood impatiently outside STIA, staring through the store window during her discussion with Evelyn Luca.

"Shit, pull over, Kevin. Xavier, I'll call you back," Sharon said, as she set her phone on the seat.

Kevin jammed on the brakes; this was not the time to ask questions. The truck and its container slid through the exit gate. Two more trucks were stacked behind, their diesel engines belching soot into the clear Oakland air, waiting for clearance.

"That first truck, Lau was in the passenger seat. She's running this whole operation. Where she goes, we go. Okay?"

"Sharon, they weren't supposed to pick the boxes up until late this afternoon; that's when they were scheduled. Why now?" Kevin said.

"Lopez says they're shutting the gates; they'll slip out before the order reaches the booths. Nethermann said they switched the container numbers; they did the same thing in Mexico. We were babysitting one set of four containers; they waltzed in and picked up these three under different manifests and schedules. The fourth, Nethermann's men just shot up; some of her men were coming into the US through the back door and got caught."

Sharon pointed at the last of the trailers leaving the port. "Kevin, we need to follow those boxes."

The three red PCL boxes, locked to their trailers, slid out the gate and onto the street. Kevin maneuvered his SUV and followed at a discreet distance. Soon the cabs were lost in the mix of traffic on 880, but their boxes were never lost from view.

"Sergeant Chang, O'Mara here," she said as she put her cell phone on speaker. "We're trailing three containers south on 880. My guess is they're not going far. Anything more at the port?"

"No, Sharon, I'm there now and Lopez just left. Nick caught a piece of shrapnel from a grenade; one of his men is down but he's okay. The illegals are all accounted for; I'll follow you as soon as I can. You need more of Oakland's finest, Lieutenant?"

Sharon smiled at the military reference; yes, this was like the old days, and she just hoped it didn't end up like the last time she trailed trucks hauling shipping containers. She didn't want this to end up like the one seriously fucked-up operation in Iraq.

Drones had trailed three containers from their entry at Husaiba down Route 12 to Ramadi; intel said they were full of contraband, a fancy three syllable word for guns and ammo. The back ends of the boxes were packed with toys and TVs. What grunt would want to spend the time pulling the junk out, leaving themselves exposed? This was not the first time she and her squad had to deal with containers. They set up a roadblock north of Ramadi. An irrigation canal protected their northern flank, flat desert left their view to the south open, and three Humvees blocked the road. O'Mara put five man teams to each side. The tractor trailers slid to a stop; the drivers waved their papers at the troops. Three of her men were new, and she could not stop them before they started to walk up to the cabs. The driver of the first truck pulled a pistol from his lap and fired at the three. One went down, a bullet to his face; the others were hit in the legs. Immediately behind the first trailer, the other drivers dismounted and fired at the squad with AK-47s. To Sharon's shock, the side of the second container opened and three men jumped to the ground, RPGs instantly thrown to their shoulders.

"Shit, down," Sharon screamed. Two of the RPGs were fired off and flew over the Humvees. The third man, as he brought his to bear on the lead truck, was cut in two by the .50 caliber mounted on the second Humvee. The corporal raked the other two before they could find cover. Sharon watched the three men to each side of the trucks open up on the cabs; the windows on the first two exploded, their drivers cut to shreds. The last cab sat smoldering.

"I want no man near that truck for five minutes." She could hear the man screaming in the cab, begging for help, in English. "No man moves near that truck. Corporal, swing that gun around and cover that cab." The corporal did as he was told.

"I see no one in the cab, Lieutenant. Just screaming—no body." Sharon's radio sounded scratchy.

"You hold. Do you hear me, Private? I want an affirmative."

"Yes, ma'am, holding."

Silence. The screaming stopped. No noise from the trucks— just the goddamn incessant wind from somewhere in the hot heart of the desert. The corporal slowly dismounted and joined the driver behind the Humvee; they put their hands over their ears. Five seconds passed. O'Mara and the other Army cops put the first two trailers between them in the last container.

"Allahu Akbar, Allahu Akbar," the screaming began from the last cab. Before the Arabic phrase "God is great" could be screamed again, the cab exploded throwing shrapnel and truck parts across the highway.

"Fucker deserved what he got," was all O'Mara offered as she assessed the damage from the screwed-up roadblock. One of her men dead, been in Iraq just two weeks; two with busted legs, but would walk again; three containers with five hundred AK-47s, fifty RPGs, boxes of mines, and thousands of rounds and six dead Al-Qaeda—five could be identified; the one who blew himself up was only known to Allah. The toy boxes and TVs were all fakes.

"Danny, I spotted Lau leaving the port as we entered; she has to be with the containers. The boxes Homeland was watching were not the real ones. Nick says the numbers were changed; my guess is they were switched on the ship. We are following at a distance, will keep you posted."

"What about Lopez?" Kevin asked.

Sharon looked out the back of the car and saw Lopez in the

windshield of his Humvee; he was one car behind them. She called.

"That was Doris Lau in the cab of the first truck, Xavier. We are following her. The boxes in the port were the wrong ones and these are the right ones."

"At least you could have called, Sharon."

"Couldn't, was talking to Chang; I see you. Watch your driving."

"Señorita O'Mara, such a nice day for a tour of the back alleys of Oakland; gracias, and where do you think they're going?" Lopez said.

"Watch and wait. I don't think they're going very far. Mostly everything south of here is warehouse or industrial complexes. Be ready to call your buddies at Homeland as soon as we turn off. We'll hold back. In fact, let's split up; we don't want to cause suspicion. I will get off at the next exit after they leave the freeway. You follow further back; your Humvee is too conspicuous. You call me after you call the Feds and I'll backtrack to you."

"Si, I understand." Lopez hung up.

Sharon and Kevin followed about a thousand yards behind the last truck. At the High Street exit, the three trailers left 880. They stopped at High Street, then continued south and paralleled the freeway for almost two miles, they watched the four trucks head toward the Oakland airport. They held back as long as they could before the traffic pushed them past the lead truck. Sharon ducked down just in case a sideways look might give them away; one man, in a ubiquitous SUV, would not draw attention. She lost them as they approached Hegenberger; her phone buzzed.

"According to the fancy GPS, they're turning on to Roland and heading toward Edgewater," Lopez said. "She has a lot of balls; we're passing the Alameda Superior Court building."

"We'll get off on Hegenberger, then backtrack to you. You think they're heading somewhere near you?"

"Probably. The map says there's not much more toward the airport. Their final destination must be near here. They're turning again; good chance for a warehouse around here. I have passed three other container and trailer rigs, stuff coming and going; they would be lost in the traffic. I'll hold back; I'm way too obvious."

The three rigs disappeared around a corner. When they reached the corner, all three were gone, like they had disappeared into thin air.

"What the hell?" was all Lopez heard from O'Mara.

"What?"

"Gone. They pulled into a building somewhere around here, well done, no lining up, and no waiting. They must have easy drive-in access into one of these buildings and called ahead to have the doors open. There's nothing here but warehouses and businesses. Where are you?"

"I'm waiting at the courthouse."

"I know this area well, Sharon, from my old Oakland days. Used to be a couple of good bars around here; we'll talk about that later."

She smiled. "I can't wait. What do you think?"

"Lots of opportunities. My guess is they won't have a big sign out front that says 'China Imports' on it."

"I see you," Lopez said.

"Let's just pass each other and then casually drive around looking for something to pop out at us. They have to be in one of the larger buildings to get all those trucks in," Sharon said.

"Si."

By process of elimination, they figured that it had to be one of five buildings; three had a lot of glass on their fronts. Sharon nixed those. "Too vulnerable."

That left two others, a newer steel-sided building and another older concrete block building, which had large roll-up doors and no windows. The faded sign said "Bright Laundry."

"You don't think they would use an old Chinese laundry; do you, Kevin?"

"Why not hide in plain sight? From a strategic point of view, the building looks solid. Did you see the high cameras? Nothing is missed. Make sure Lopez doesn't drive by again. My guess is that if they spot him making more than one pass, they will get a bit edgy."

Sharon passed on the information; they agreed to rendez-vous in the parking lot of the Superior Court.

Lopez pulled in directly behind them. Lopez was on the phone.

"Si, I think we know where they are . . . Si, si, no, they didn't see us . . . at least I don't think so . . . si, we will stay here. Hope-fully they're unloading and don't have a clue."

With Lopez's conversation over, he smiled at her. "Well, Señorita, what do you think?"

For a long moment she looked at the two big men, then, be-tween their shoulders, she watched as five black Cadillac Esca-lades roared down Edgewater toward the warehouse.

"My guess is that's some of your countrymen, Xavier. They may be trying to beat us to the party. If I haven't seen a gang caravan just go by, then I don't know what I just saw. Mount up, boys, this ain't gonna be pretty!"

15b

The major, and most obvious, difference between the Iraqi gangs and the Mexican cartels was their transportation. Escalades versus Toyota pickups with machine guns mounted on their beds. Bulletproof and well-armored hundred-thousand-dollar SUVs versus nothing but firepower and a strong belief in a life after death with a bunch of virgins. Other than that, they were almost the same—both used the knife to coerce information and both were known for their total lack of morality or honor. Honor among thieves happened only in the movies. These gangs would cut your throat for a "Forever" postage stamp.

Sharon and Kevin climbed into Lopez's Humvee; they left the Superior Court parking lot, and followed the Escalades; sur-prise was not something that could be counted on now. They turned into the lot across the street from the laundry. "Let's see what happens," Sharon said.

Two of the SUVs pulled into the parking lot along the side of the laundry. Four men bailed out—the last two held RPGs. Two banks of roll-up doors faced the lot. One man casually walked out from behind the SUV and raised his RPG; the door was fifty feet way. The other men pulled out AR-15s and took positions in front of the other black SUV.

The other two Escalades had passed the building and were now covering the far side. Eight men took cover behind the SUVs. No RPGs, but enough weaponry to fight a skirmish in Baghdad. O'Mara and Lopez recognized the Barrett M-107 carried by one man; he set it up on the hood of the car.

"Nice hood ornament," she said.

"Yeah, that would certainly help you get through traffic," Lopez added.

"Are we just gonna stand here?" Kevin asked.

"Well, I sure as hell am not going to try and get in their way," Lopez said. "Those assholes want to kill each other; it's okay by me."

"Kevin, you know one of those boxes may have young girls in it, and God knows what else. If they unload, the whole building could go up. We need to try and do something," Sharon said, hoping for a miracle.

The miracle came from the roof. In less than a second, four men stood, RPGs to their shoulders, and fired at the pride of General Motors. The explosions blew the SUVs to pieces and knocked down all the Mexicans, including the men with the RPGs. The man with the Barrett disappeared in a flash, the rifle nothing more than impotent steel. Instantly, after the RPGs, three more men raked the smoking hulks with automatic weapons; from the sound, Sharon recognized that they were AK-47s. In five seconds, nothing moved. The men walked the parapet watching for movement; the sound of sirens started to fill the shallow canyons between the buildings.

"If you're going to shoot, shoot. If not, you're going to die," Lopez said, pointing to the Escalades. "Old Mexican proverb."

Their small group was three hundred feet from the explosions and the gunfire, not entirely hidden. One man stood on the roof, his bald head flaring in the late afternoon sun. He scanned the lot and the street and then spotted the four. He raised the rifle to his shoulder.

"Hit the deck," Sharon yelled, as three quick rounds hit Lopez's Humvee. Kevin rolled behind the SUV. "Inspector, I hope you have insurance."

"It's a government rental, your government," Lopez added with a laugh. "Everyone okay?"

No one was hit or even nicked. The man on the roof, along with the others, disappeared as fast as he appeared. Three black Escalades were burning; every cartel soldier was down and, from every direction, sirens and blue and red lights began to flash.

Before the first Oakland squad cars pulled onto Edgewater, one of the roll-up doors quickly opened and two step-vans exploded out of the building with "Bright Laundry" painted on their sides. At the street, they split in two directions. Sharon watched the first driver try to jam his way through the oncoming squad cars; he managed to pass the first two, and the third police car spun across his path and absorbed the full impact of the van. The other squad cars opened fire on the truck; the rear doors flew open and five men jumped out, firing wildly, using the van for cover.

Sharon turned and watched the other van drive head-on into an oncoming armored personnel vehicle, with "OPD" painted on its side. The Oakland police won. No one jumped out of the back of the van. She thought, *At the speed they were going, anyone standing would be plastered against the interior walls of the van.* The driver, she was sure, should have gone through the window; she guessed he didn't have his seat belt on, another safety violation.

The scene at the first laundry van was under control quickly, with two on the ground, and the others with their hands up. The Oakland cops all held AR-15s; this was not the police of twenty years ago. Two Army National Guard Hueys circled overhead.

Danny Chang waved toward the three in the lot.

"You guys okay? It looked like World War III here when we pulled in."

"Seen worse in Iraq," Sharon answered. "But this isn't Iraq and this should not happen here—too much firepower for a bunch of gangs and thugs, way too much."

"I agree," Chang said. "But this is what's happening with all these arms coming in covertly through here. They probably end up in Mexico."

"And my country thanks you for that!" Lopez added, as he lit a cigar. Sharon was already into her second Marlboro. "All this crap comes through these ports and in those damn boxes. Then they are smuggled over the border and my people suffer. It's a son of a bitch."

15c

Within minutes, over one hundred police and guardsmen converged on the warehouse; not another shot was fired.

"And what did the three of you have to do with all this?" Chang said, pointing over his shoulder.

"Well, Officer, we were just standing here having a pleasant conversation about Mexican trade and the effects of currency revaluation and these four black cars pulled up to that building over there and then, Officer, well, all hell sort'a exploded all around us." Sharon used her best southern drawl she had picked up from one of her men in Iraq.

Danny broke into a smile. "At least you're not hurt. With all the crap flying around, I'm surprised someone outside this blast zone wasn't at least injured; Oakland was lucky." Chang's phone rang to the tune of the Lone Ranger theme song. "Homeland, just a minute."

Chang walked away from the group, phone to his ear. He stood with his hand on his weapon. He stared at the scene while he talked. After thirty seconds, he walked back to the three.

"They've swept the building clean. No hostiles; everyone must have been in the two vans. They said they want me to come in and translate—seems they found survivors in one of the containers, all from China."

"More girls. Is Jiao with them?" Sharon asked.

"Seems so, the goddamn bastards. Mom and Mei will be happy," Chang said.

"Did they find Lau?"

"No word."

The four walked across the street and between the squad cars that now filled the parking lot; Chang left them for a moment to talk with the SWAT team that had just arrived. Fire trucks had arrived to douse the flames billowing out of the Escalades. It was chaos in black and white, and red and blue. Medical teams from the coroner's office were beginning to process the bodies, and look for IDs or anything else that would help identify the men sprawled in the parking lot and on the street.

Sergeant Chang walked up to the three. "Latest body count, we have twelve Mexicans down, ten are dead, and two are badly wounded. The Chinese left two on the street, three wounded over there. In the van that hit the APV, four are pretty busted up, but should live. My men are collecting weapons; there's enough to arm a platoon of soldiers in Iraq. Shit, this is what we're dealing with now on the streets: RPGs, Barretts, AR-15s, M-4s, AK-47s, fuck." Chang walked toward the roll-up door. In the darkness, Sharon could see the tractor-trailer rigs and the containers still locked to the flatbeds. The doors to all the boxes were open.

"Sergeant Chang, they want you at the last one. The other containers are secured." The young patrolman pointed toward the large forty-foot red box with *PCL* painted on its side.

Sharon looked where the cop pointed; she thought about blue seas and the near miss the last time she saw one of these up close. Medical personnel were entering and leaving the container; a ladder had been propped against the edge of the trailer deck. She watched Chang climb up and enter the box.

"What do you think, Sharon? Hopefully, it's not as bad as the last time you opened one of these cursed things," Lopez said, without any humor. "I'm beginning to think these are all the devil's making; seems like nothing good is found in them."

"My boat captain in Cabo said that when they are opened, it's like Christmas—you never know what's inside. I understand where you're coming from, Xavier. Want some coffee, Kevin?"

"You and your damn coffee, Sharon. Sure, I'll have a cup. In fact, there's a Starbucks just a few blocks from here, and I'll drive. Besides, I need to use the can," Kevin said. "Lopez?"

"Si, take the truck, I'll stay here. Homeland and your Feds will be all over this in an hour; Sergeant Chang will be thrilled. I'll have a large black, thanks Kevin. See you shortly, Señorita." Lopez smiled at the redhead, a flirtatious smile, hardly the leer she first saw as he walked the beach in Mexico.

"Back in a minute! Don't do anything rash."

They crossed Edgewater to the Humvee. The Starbucks was about four blocks away, but they had to take a circuitous route, now that patrol cars and federal vehicles filled the streets. They passed by people standing in front of their offices and warehouses; everyone wanted to know what was going on. The sky now held four choppers; the Hueys were gone. They were replaced with the various news helicopters from the regional stations, radio and TV.

Their route circled the block that held the Bright Laundry building and they were soon paralleling 880; the thick SUV windows deadened the noise from the freeway.

"We were lucky."

"Damn lucky," Sharon answered.

The SUV pulled up to a stop sign. To their right, Sharon saw the flashing lights of the small army that filled Edgewater. A row of small warehouses faced the freeway and, to their surprise, the first building's roll-up door began to slide open. They watched as the nose of a step-van tentatively appeared, like a rat sticking its snout out of its hole. Then the whole van slid into view, "Bright Laundry" painted on its side. It sat as if waiting for something. The something was a tall bald Chinaman dressed in black. He walked down the side of the van, the roll-up slowly closing behind him; an AK-47 was gripped tightly in his hand.

"That's the son of a bitch from the roof," Kevin said.

"Couldn't mistake that asshole's face anywhere. Now what?"

"My guess is that Lau's in that van. They must have figured a way to get to this building during the firefight. They have a straight shot to the freeway from here; as slippery as they've been, they could be gone in seconds. What do you think?"

"Well, let's see. I have Lopez's M-4 on the floor behind me and two clips for my pistol. My guess is you have a clip for your Beretta and that's it. Based on what I saw in that warehouse, they just may have a small tank hidden in that van. Well?"

Sharon looked at Kevin and smiled. "What the fuck?"

The "what the fuck" was answered when Doris Lau's pink hair popped up in the window on the driver's side.

"Buckle up. If you hit her in the driver side and continue to accelerate, then maybe we can overturn it. If you hit the driver's door, maybe it'll knock'em out."

"That's your plan? Run into them, ram them!" He looked at her. "I like it, I really like it. Close your eyes when the air bags go off because we'll be blinded for a second; wait, I'll shut yours off." Kevin clicked the car seat switch, shutting off the left air bag. "Get ready."

Cinched in, they watched as the van slowly rolled down the ramp from the warehouse. When it reached the sidewalk, Kevin floored the huge V-8 and the SUV lunged from the stop sign, like it had been kicked in the ass; even through the firewall sound insulation, the noise was deafening.

The van passed the curb; she glanced at the readout on the SUV's dash, and it said 48 in large luminous numbers. "Shit," was all that he heard.

It took three seconds for the vehicles to collide; their embrace was not gentle. Kevin succeeded in catching the side panel of the driver's door with his right bumper; the collision was not head-on and that's what he hoped would not happen. She knew a forceful glancing blow would spin the van and maybe even flip it. She was partially correct. The door caved in, she saw another flash of pink through the window, and the woman flew like a doll being thrown against a wall. The van tipped to one side and stood high on its right side for a moment, like it was trying to decide which way to fall, before crashing back to the street. With no driver in control, its momentum continued to roll it down the street. Kevin continued to push the SUV into the forward corner of the van until it clipped a hydrant. The van jerked to a stop over the exploding fountain of water. The water, forced horizontal like a hand over a vertical shaft of high-pressure water, sprayed in all directions from under the truck. They bailed from the Humvee as soon as he could back it away from the truck; Kevin pulled the M-4 from the back seat. Her weapon was already in her hand. They moved cautiously toward the new water feature visible from the 880 freeway; cars were already beginning to back up, gawkers.

Sharon watched Lau rounded the back of the van. Blood ran from a crack in her forehead; the spray from the hydrant washed it away as fast as it appeared. Lau held a pistol in her left hand.

Shocked at seeing O'Mara, all she could scream was, "You!" She raised her arm to shoot. Sharon, her Beretta already at shoulder height, fired two rounds, both striking Lau in the upper right shoulder, spinning Lau to the gutter.

"Kevin, left!"

He looked hard left and watched Feng turn the corner of the crushed laundry truck, his AK-47 rising. Kevin, never one to ponder shooting conditions, swung the M-4 to his shoulder and fired, or at least tried—the safety was still locked. Pushing the safety off, he was a half second late; Feng's round whizzed past his ear. A second shot, behind and to his right, exploded in his ear. Through his gun sight, he saw Feng stagger; another shot from Sharon hit him again, and the AK-47 dropped, through the spray, to the pavement. Feng, a look of hatred hardened on his face, had still not felt the pain. Losing all functions, he collapsed into the torrent of water coursing down the street; the hydrant's spray diluted the blood that pumped into the gutter as his exploded heart shut down.

Epilogue

The Backyard Dinner Party

Sharon wondered what was in the huge box delivered by Federal Express. It was almost ten feet long, twelve inches thick, and twenty inches deep; all it said on the outside was her name and address and, in bold letters, "NO ABRA" in Spanish, and in English "DO NOT OPEN." In small text a short note said, "Wait for the party, Xavier." For two days, it had sat in her living room. Basil immediately sniffed its length, harrumphed, curled up on his bed, and ignored it. She could not ignore it; it WAS the eight-hundred-pound gorilla in the room.

The party was at four, the weather clear and sunny, and the heat of summer was a week away. She set up long folding tables in the backyard, colorful tablecloths spread along them with an eclectic collection of plastic plates, cups, and wineglasses. Chairs had been rented and delivered. Basil sniffed everything and strolled about in anticipation.

During the five days since the capture of Lau and the collapse of her family's business in Oakland, much had been accomplished and many questions had been answered. Deng Jiao was discovered in one of the containers, along with the ten other girls, and all were well. They had recovered enough to be questioned about their ordeal. Seven wanted to return home, and three were seeking some form of compassionate asylum and help. Jiao was living with Norma Chang and Mei, and their reunion brought tears even to Sharon. Jiao hoped to stay in America since there was nowhere else for her to call home.

The men that were discovered in the other box were the unfortunate result of a port screw-up. Even though the false paperwork was correct, the box had been misread by the trailer driver and, when he dropped the box for the gantry operator, one more snafu was added to the confusion, and it was stacked in the wrong place—only Nethermann's doggedness had found the box, resulting in the firefight. Vaca was doing well, and could walk with a cane; Vaca and Nethermann were awarded Purple Hearts. The men in the box were labeled terrorists by Homeland; two were hustled away and out of the country, location unknown. The Feds announced that another terrorist plot had been foiled, as a result of international cooperation; Detective Inspector Lopez posed with a big Peron smile in all the photos.

The other containers held a bizarre mixture of weapons, fake merchandise, clothing, counterfeit Euros, and handbags. Customs officials paraded out the goods on long tables in the captured laundry warehouse; for all intents and purposes, it looked like a sidewalk sale. One cynical writer, for the *Contra Costa Times*, called it exactly that in its headline, "Homeland Defense's Flea Market."

Lau rolled on everyone when she was threatened with Gitmo; she told them she was an American. They just rolled their eyes and said, "And we believe you?"

Thaddeus Spinos was arrested at his suburban Lafayette tract home, during a backyard barbeque; Lau had been invited but could not attend due to a previous engagement. She had passed on her invitation to Kevin Bryan, who led the raid; Sergeant Chang tagged along. Spinos collapsed during the interview—seems he had partied a bit too much and took an overdose.

Gina Cavelli was the first to arrive. When Sharon stopped by for a post-Oakland mayhem drink, she was the first to hear the end of the story that had started in Mexico. She suggested the party and offered her bartending services, as long as there was Mexican food and no goddamn Mojitos. When Sharon suggested expanding the menu, to include Chinese and Italian, she was locked in. She proceeded to set up the bar in the backyard.

The Changs were next. Norma escorted the two girls and Danny carried steaming aluminum trays. Sharon watched the girls walk through the cottage and smiled—they were such beautiful young women, bright, curious, and tall, and, above all, teenagers. Their trials of the last few months would roll off these country girls like the latest fad. Norma had told her they were already enrolled in high school and their aptitude tests were scheduled for the week after next; she knew they would succeed.

Kevin arrived carrying large bags of ice, and, after dumping them in the cooler next to Gina, brought in sacks of salad and vegetables; he busied himself in the kitchen setting up trays of hors d'oeuvres. Gina delivered an iced Jameson to him and set it next to him on the counter—a quick kiss was offered as a bonus. Sharon walked through the kitchen and kissed him on the other cheek.

"You ready for this crowd?" Kevin asked, a stick of celery in the corner of his mouth.

"For this crowd, absolutely ready," she answered.

Evelyn carried three bags through the kitchen door. "I know where to put these, or at least I should. Sharon?"

"Evelyn." She quickly brushed Luca's cheek. "There, there, and there." Sharon watched as Mei carried a fabulously wrapped package through the kitchen and out into the backyard. "What was that?"

"Never mind; I need to heat the lasagna and prep the Alfredo. Kevin, bread?"

"In the bag."

Norma pushed her way through the growing crowd. "Kevin, there are two trays of pork buns and pot stickers that need to be warmed. Where?"

"Ask Sharon."

"I did. She said you know where; she's talking with the girls; Danny's translating—ought to be fun to listen to."

"The grill is warm; can you do them on the grill? Gina will show you where."

"I'll make it work." Norma turned to Evelyn. "I'm Norma Chang."

"I'm Evelyn Luca. You're taking care of the girls, and that's wonderful."

"Yes, they were lucky, very lucky."

"There're a lot of lucky people here this afternoon."

From down the hall came a loud banging, followed by swearing in Spanish, second best only to Italian cursing. Nick Nethermann pushed his way into the kitchen, followed by Detective Inspector Xavier Immanuel Lopez carrying a huge aluminum foil tray. The aromas of cilantro and tomatillos filled the air.

Sharon looked through the kitchen window and spied Lopez. She waved, and he yelled, "Where?"

"There," she said, pointing to the table just outside the door.

"Sergeant, there's beer or something stronger over at the bar, see Gina," Kevin said over his shoulder, the celery still stuck in his cheek. "Lopez, she has beer and anything else you might want."

Lopez looked out the door to the setup where Gina was working. "Detective Bryan, who is that gorgeous woman at the bar?" Kevin could only roll his eyes and look at the ceiling.

Sharon gave Lopez a kiss and a hug; Lopez tried to linger a bit. "Xavier, this is Gina Cavelli, an old friend and confidante, she also owns the best bar in the county."

Lopez smiled and bowed, as only a Mexican aristocrat could. Gina smiled and winked at Sharon. Sharon mouthed, "Be careful!" to Gina, who laughed out loud.

"What? Did I say somethings?" Lopez said, looking curiously. Cavelli laughed again.

Jazz floated through the afternoon and filled the bits and spaces left open by the aromas from the food. The large table was piled high with a wondrous collection of foods from around the world, each more delectable than the last—a bite of lasagna, followed by enchiladas suizas, and finishing with a Chinese pork dish, lost in translation but the first tray to be emptied.

A bottle of brandy floated around the table. Norma allowed the girls a sip, but was clearly glad they coughed and tittered away after the attempt; the table toasted to their future and their potential. They blushed as Norma translated Kevin's comments.

Nick Nethermann stood and offered a short toast to Sharon; he shyly pointed out that it was her tenacity that kept much of this moving forward.

Evelyn stood and motioned to Mei; she found the package and, at Luca's direction, handed it to Sharon. "Sharon dear, it has been a bizarre and difficult spring, but, through your efforts, I have a cleaner and better business and my family wants to thank you. Please." She motioned to Sharon and the package.

She held the box, with its incredible wrapping of gilded paper and ribbon; she looked at Evelyn and said, "How?"

"Come on, girl, you've never opened a gift? Rip it."

She pulled the ribbon and peeled back the paper; a cedar box emerged. Clicking back the lock, she opened the lid and found a red silk bag; opening the bag, she withdrew a leather handbag that glowed in the late afternoon sunshine. A subtle texture worked its way through the leather; the clasps and buckles were like jewelry. Its softness could be seen as well as felt. Jiao started to clap, and within a second the whole table was applauding.

"Sharon, it's the first of the new line; my father wanted you to have it."

"Evelyn dear," Sharon said, caressing the bag, "I have nothing to wear with this, nothing."

"I know, Sharon; oh, how I know." The table erupted with laughter.

Sharon smiled at the table and noticed Kevin and Nethermann were missing. Looking into the kitchen, she heard Basil's deep barking as he bounded through the door, immediately followed by the two men. Between them, they carried the huge FedEx carton. Lopez stood.

"Señors, Señoras, and Señoritas, this young lady has caused my government and my people a lot of grief since she visited my country. She had come to my country for the sun and the fish, to drink good beer, and to relax. All she found was a container filled with death, purses . . ."

"Handbags," corrected Luca.

"Pardon, handbags, and Lord knows what else. We will never know because she conveniently caused an earthquake and a tidal wave to wash it all away. Then, here in her home country, she gets involved with the Chinese Tong and the Mexican cartels, guns, and kidnapped young ladies, who, due to the efforts of her and others, saved them from evil." Lopez smiled at the two young girls; Norma was translating. They returned his smile.

"So, Señorita Sharon O'Mara, one of the unrequited loves of my life, I give you this not-so-small token of my country and my fondness for you. Please, Sharon. Nick, can you help?"

Nethermann extracted a clasp knife from his pocket, opened it, and handed it to Sharon. She took a tentative slice at the tape, and then, under everyone's encouragement, opened the rest of the lid. Tissue and Styrofoam bits filled the box; she pushed aside the materials and let out an, "Oh my God, Xavier, no. Can you help?"

Nethermann and Kevin each reached inside and grasped an end and raised up the most spectacular black marlin mount Sharon had ever seen. The colors glowed in the sun, the dorsal fin erect; its eye challenged everyone who stared at it.

"I talked with Gregorio and he described the black marlin you released just before you found the container. This is a cast that they make for those that want a copy of the fish they caught and released. Its original was five hundred and twenty-five pounds, which is what Gregorio says your fish weighed. She is magnificent, is she not?" Lopez pointed at the fish and Sharon.

Basil barked and then harrumphed.

Sharon O'Mara, for one of the few times in her life, was speechless.

THE END

A Note from the Author
The Flyer

I have tried to pare these stories into a manageable length that you can read in less than eight hours. At about 60–75,000 words, the idea is that you can read about half the book on a four-hour flight and the rest on the way home. I call them *Flyers*. But if you aren't flying, settle back, pour a good drink, and enjoy.

Gregory C. Randall was born in Traverse City, Michigan. He grew up in Chicago. Greg has never forgotten his roots. Mr. Randall makes his home in California.

Mr. Randall is the author of fiction and nonfiction works available through Amazon.com.

For more information about the other Sharon O'Mara Chronicles, and planned sequels, please visit and connect with Greg online:

www.gregorycrandall.info

See his blogs:
http://www.writing4death.blogspot.com

Other books by Mr. Randall:
Fiction
The Cherry Pickers

The Sharon O'Mara Chronicles
Land Swap For Death
Containers For Death
Toulouse For Death
12th Man For Death
Diamonds For Death
Limerick For Death

The Alex Polonia Thrillers
Venice Black
Saigon Red
St. Petersburg White

The Tony Alfano Thrillers
Chicago Swing
Chicago Jazz
Chicago Fix
Chicago Boogie Woogie

Max Adler OSS WWII
This Face of Evil
Pawns in an Ancient Game

Science Fiction and Slipstream
Sector 73
Seven Hours to Barstow

Nonfiction
America's Original GI Town, Park Forest, Illinois

Additional copies can be purchased through Amazon.coms.